She moved past him and looked down at the body of
Matthew Bowman, who floated face up in the water, one arm half
wrapped around a pylon as though he were trying to anchor himself.
But it was purely chance because Bowman wouldn't have been
trying to do anything after having his heart turned to ash. The gaping
hole in his chest looked almost cauterized. "Fire spell?" she asked
quietly.

Poorhouse shrugged. "Could be a salamander. The forensic
people should be able to tell us something once they've had a look at
him."

MANAGANSETT PRESS

THE MALTESE GARGOYLE

Don D'Ammassa

Dashiell Hammett was one of the most influential writers of all time. I would like to think that this playful pastiche would amuse him.

Managansett Press Edition 2015

THE MALTESE GARGOYLE

CHAPTER ONE

Wanda Coyne was not a beautiful woman, but there was something striking in her appearance that had held the eyes and interest of many a man and more than a few women. Her features were sharply chiseled, a high definition face in a low definition world. Dark brown hair barely reached her shoulders and her eyes were capable of generating such intensity that some of her clients thought she just might be demonically possessed even though she was not licensed for paranormal enhancements. Her office was functional with nothing to let a visitor acquire any insights into its owner. She liked it that way, which was something of an insight in itself. The furniture was old and showed signs of wear, but the marks resulted from use rather than abuse. Wanda didn't mind using things up, but she detested waste. An omniscient observer would have noticed that the dingy conditions were not a sign of failure so much as indifference.

Wanda had been staring at the office wall for some time that morning. Her features were immobile but her thoughts danced nimbly although they could never quite assert any influence over her expression. She glanced up as Perry Everdeen stuck his head through the door of her office. "Yes, what is it?"

It was a handsome head, crested with wheat blonde hair. Perry insisted on wearing a suit to work and he looked good in it. Wanda admired the effect but only academically. Perry was a few years younger than she physically and considerably more than that experientially. It was not entirely clear to her how Perry regarded the relationship between the two of them, but since it was not entirely clear to him either, this was hardly surprising. He glanced back into the outer office, then slipped inside, closing the door after him.

"There's a young lady here to see you. She didn't have an appointment. Do you want to talk to her?"

"Since we're not exactly overflowing with clients, I think I can fit her in. What's her name?"

"Crest. Miss Marvella Crest."

Perry disappeared briefly, then returned to usher Marvella Crest into Wanda's presence. She was a tiny woman who looked to be barely out of her teens with a pale complexion like well polished porcelain. She wore her quite expensive clothes like a department store manikin; she had arranged them on her body rather than dressed herself, which seemed a contradiction based on the elaborate care with which she had applied her makeup. Wanda rose and reached across the desk to shake hands, and felt a cool, damp palm against hers. Her visitor was ill at ease, seemed ready to bolt.

"Please sit down, Miss Crest."

The young woman took her time doing so, possibly using the extra seconds to gather her resolve. Possibly conducting a surreptitious evaluation of her surroundings. Wanda employed the time by watching her potential client closely. It was too early to draw conclusions, but she had a working hypothesis. Crest was not used to managing things for herself and wasn't quite certain how to go about it. She had had money in the past though not perhaps at present, either from a family or a patron, but she probably hadn't been born to it. It was obvious that she was having second thoughts and that she had only come in the first place because she was desperate. There was no wedding ring. Blackmail was most likely the problem, perhaps a love affair that had gone bad. She was apprehensive, but there was steel there as well. She was more formidable than her appearance and behavior suggested. Wanda had initially been afraid that she might panic the girl if she pushed too soon, but revised her opinion quickly. There was determination there as well as deliberation. Wanda waited patiently while her visitor tried to decide whether or not to cross her legs. Crest was attempt to project a particular image, but she hadn't thought through the details and was improvising.

Crest was also wearing charm bracelets on both wrists, obviously expensive ones, but Wanda couldn't see them clearly enough to divine their purpose. Good luck tokens were so common now that they cancelled each other out, but if you were willing to spend enough money, you could still buy custom made charms that influenced specific situations – better seating at public events, expedited service at government offices, a mild enhancement of one's sexual allure, etc. Most people still bought a variety of the less ineffective ones because they feared that if they failed to do so, all of

the bad luck that had been magically thwarted would eventually have
to settle on anyone unprotected. It wasn't true, but you couldn't argue
with blind faith.

The silence stretched and Wanda shifted position, sitting
back in as non-threatening a pose as she could manage. "This office
is snooper warded, Miss Crest. You can speak freely here. Even
though you're not yet a client, whatever you might wish to say to me
will be kept confidential. I wouldn't have stayed in business as long
as I have if I was indiscrete or unprotected."

"Yes, I'm sorry. This is very difficult for me. I'm really not
sure how to start."

"Try the beginning. That usually works best."

There was a prolonged silence and Wanda was about to prod
again when Crest pressed her knees together, straightened her
shoulders, and raised her eyes. "It's my brother, my younger brother
Cory. I was supposed to look out for him while my parents were
visiting Faerie but he seemed to know what he was doing and I
really couldn't follow him around all the time to make sure he wasn't
in trouble. He's always been much more outgoing than I am and it
was obvious that he resented it even when I just asked about what he
was doing in the city. It's not as if I was trying to pry or anything like
that."

There was another prolonged silence. "Which city would this
be?" Wanda prompted.

"Here in Boston. At first I thought he just had a girlfriend and
that he wanted to keep secret for the time being so I didn't press him
for details. But then I found out he'd been dating a succubus and I
didn't know what to do. I tried to talk to him, told him we could get
counseling and break the addiction, but he got furious with me and I
decided to give him time to calm down before I tried again and then
I got the letter and I don't know what I'm going to tell Mom and Dad
when they get back." She ran out of steam then and her eyes
dropped.

"He ran off with the succubus?"

She nodded her head and there was a hint of tears in her eyes.
"The letter said that he was happier than he'd ever been in his life
and that he wasn't going to let anyone spoil it for him. I didn't know
what to do so I came east to look for him but his apartment is empty

and no knows or will admit they know where he's gone. Dad will blame me for it; I know he will."

"When are your parents due back?"

"Two weeks from today. They're taking the full tour."

"And you have no idea where your brother might have gone?"

She shook her head. "He didn't leave a forwarding address and when I tried to hire a Locator, she said there were too many auras in Boston to find one individual unless he was carrying a sigil or something else that would stand out. I put an ad in the local papers and someone who claimed he was Cory's friend came to see me and told me that I should go home, that Cory didn't want to see me just now. I begged him to tell me where Cory was but he refused."

"Did he give you his name?"

"Thursday. Lloyd Thursday. He said that Cory was happy and safe and that I shouldn't worry about him, that he would get in touch when he felt he could trust me again. But he wouldn't look at me while he was talking and I think he was lying. Don't you?"

Wanda made a noncommittal noise. "I don't know enough yet to have an opinion but he might have been telling the truth." But probably not. Affairs with succubi were intensely pleasurable but they rarely ended well. Except maybe for the succubi.

"I told him that I wasn't going anywhere until I spoke to Cory himself and he got very angry with me and told me that I was interfering where I wasn't wanted. He didn't actually threaten me but it felt that way and I thought about changing hotels so he couldn't find me again, but if I did that and he really was my only link to Cory, then I couldn't do that either, could I?"

"No, of course not."

"So I asked him to take a message to my brother and bring me the answer tonight. I had planned to decide what to do after I heard what Cory had to say, but since then I realized that I can't do that. I mean, what if this man just makes something up? I suppose I could have demanded the answer to some question only Cory and I would know but it didn't occur to me at the time. And even if he had proof that Cory had gone away of his own free will, I can't just leave my brother in thrall to a succubus, can I?"

"No, of course not." Free will was a nebulous legal concept. Wanda was perfectly willing to interpret it differently in different situations.

"Then you'll help me?" Crest suddenly opened her purse and took out a roll of bills coiled inside a rubber band. "Will five hundred dollars be enough? It's all I have."

"That's enough for now. Where are you supposed to meet Mr.Thursday?"

"In the dining room at my hotel. I thought it should be some place public. I don't trust him."

"I don't blame you. Is it all right if I bring my partner in and tell him your story? " Crest looked uncertain. "I'm committed to another case this evening and Matthew has more experience tailing people than I do."

"Okay. I guess that makes sense."

Wanda pressed the buzzer on her desk. "Matt, can you come in here for a minute?"

A few seconds later the door opened and Matthew Bowman entered the room. He wasn't quite old enough to be Wanda's father, but he was in the neighborhood. He was also the closest thing to a parent she'd ever had and he was still the senior partner in the firm, at least in theory. Bowman was winding down. He'd endured too many boring stakeouts, dealt with too many angry, philandering husbands and wives, and had run afoul of too many crooked cops, politicians, and unpleasant people in general. Inertia and his affection for Wanda kept him working after a fashion, but his heart hadn't been in the job for years. Unfortunately, he had no real life outside the job either, and if he ever retired, he'd be a basket case within a week.

Wanda summarized their new client's problem and Bowman nodded and turned to Crest. "Assuming this Thursday character shows up, it should be a simple matter to follow him afterwards. Sooner or later he'll lead us to your brother and we can figure out the next step once we know where he is." Bowman had adopted his avuncular demeanor and Crest had almost relaxed.

"Just how old is Cory?" asked Wanda.

"Nineteen."

Wanda nodded as though that didn't matter. "Well, he's reached the age of consent, which presents a problem. Nothing that we can't get around. Succubi are subject to a strict code of behavior but they're so undisciplined that they rarely pay attention to the rules. And even if she's legit, we can probably get him desensitized before she can cause trouble."

"What about Thursday?" Crest bit her lip. "How would he come into this?"

"Succubi usually employ familiars," said Bowman quietly. "They cause too much of a sensation when they appear publicly so they have a human being to front for them. She might have hired him to acquire her subjects and run interference with friends and relatives."

"Don't succubi kill their partners? We don't have any back home and I never realized they could just take people away like this."

"It's not quite that simple," said Wanda. "As I said, there are rules. And it's not likely that there's any immediate danger. It takes months, sometimes years, for a succubus to seriously drain a human, and they're supposed to get regular white cell counts done and arrange for compensatory medical treatment to offset the decline. Your brother is young enough to have a lot of life force. He's not in any immediate danger unless there is something else going on."

Bowman asked for a physical description of Thursday. Crest thought for a moment, then provided one that was surprisingly detailed. "Wavy black hair, fairly long but tight against his skull as though he uses a lot of oil. Small ears, pointed like a leprechaun, but he's quite tall, at least six feet. Dark complexion, broad nose, eyes close set with busy brows, also very dark. A pencil thin moustache and a very neat goatee. His hands are large and his fingers are long and slender. He's big through the shoulders and hips, solid but not fat. I think he'd be very dangerous in a fight. There was a small scar on his nose, but I forget which side. The left, I think."

"How was he dressed when you last saw him?"

"Dark slacks, white shirt, black jacket. But that was yesterday."

"Did you notice anything else about him that was distinctive? Did he carry a cane, for example, or smoke cigarettes?"

Crest shook her head. "He had a raspy voice, like he had something caught in his throat. That's all I remember."

She looked distressed again and Bowman smiled reassuringly. "Don't worry. There won't be any trouble identifying him. I'll be watching the two of you when you meet, but you probably won't see me so don't worry about it." He asked for a few more particulars about the meeting place and time. "It's perfectly all right to be nervous; he'll expect that. But don't look around to see if you can spot me. We don't want Thursday to suspect anything."

Crest managed to look flustered, frightened, and reassured all at the same time. Bowman actually put an arm around her shoulders when he ushered her out, then returned to find Wanda counting the roll of bills.

"Sweet little lady."

"You're too old to be getting sentimental."

"No, you're the one who's too old for sentimentality. You were born too old." He glanced at the money. "Are we keeping it all?"

"If it's as simple as it appears, probably not, although I suspect she can afford it despite what she claims. On the other hand, it's never as simple as it appears."

"Are you going out to see Willett tonight?"

She nodded. "He didn't want to talk where he works so he invited me to supper."

"I'll bet his wife is thrilled to death about that."

"Willett doesn't seem the type to have wandering eyes, but then again, they almost never do."

Wanda still renewed her license every two years but she hadn't owned a car since she'd moved to Boston eight years earlier. She took a cab to the Willetts' home in Brookline, a boxy little house with a postage stamp sized lawn. It had more floor space than her apartment, but not by much, although it was considerably neater. Gladys Willett had a mouth set in a permanent frown but she made an effort to be sociable as she let Wanda in. "Nathan's not home yet. He might have missed his usual bus. It happens sometimes. He's terrible about keeping track of time. Can I get you something to drink?" She was clearly not happy about being a good hostess but was so conditioned into the rules of hospitality that she was incapable of refraining.

"I don't want to put you out."

"It's no trouble. I have gin, whiskey, brandy, and some wine. There's beer, but it's not cold."

"A brandy would be fine. No ice."

There was a tiny bar in one corner of the living room. The furnishings were of good quality but not expensive and the room was spotlessly clean. It probably wasn't for her benefit. Wanda suspected that Gladys Willett followed her husband around with a dust rag.

"Do you know Nathan through work?"

Since she wasn't sure how much Willett had told his wife, or wanted her to know, Wanda parried. "Only indirectly. This is a nice little house. How long have you lived here?" The diversion was probably obvious but Gladys showed no sign that she resented it. They discussed generalities while Wanda finished her brandy – it was peach flavored, which she abhorred – and then declined a refill. Gladys kept glancing at the wall clock and occasionally bit her lip. More than half an hour had passed and there was still no sign of her husband. She disappeared into the kitchen every few minutes to "tend to supper" and she was there when the phone rang.

Wanda could hear her side of the conversation, which was limited to short noncommittal replies, but when she was done she came out to the living room and something had changed in her demeanor. "I'm afraid you've wasted your trip." There was a faint hesitation there, as though she wasn't sure what was going on, or was sure but lying about it. Gladys was very upset, visibly trembling,and she was trying hard not to show it. "I'm sorry that you had to come out here for nothing but my husband will be staying in the city tonight. Something came up unexpectedly."

"Should I schedule another appointment?"

"I don't know. I'm sorry."

Wanda used the Willetts' phone to call a cab, but she waited out front until it showed up. The cabbie had the radio going and they were back in Boston proper when the news came on. Nathan Willett had died from gunshot wounds received late that afternoon. He'd still been alive when he'd arrived at the hospital but neither medicine nor a licensed healer could reverse the damage. There was a brief summary of Willett's career as reporter and editor of *The Boston Journal* but no details about the shooting other than that he'd been found bleeding to death in an alley not far from his office.

Forensics would retrieve the dead man's final memories since there hadn't been time for them to disperse. If this was a random mugging, the police would probably develop a picture of the assailant's face. It might just be coincidental that Willett had asked for a meeting the same day he'd been killed, but Wanda didn't believe in coincidences. She doubted the official investigation would find anything. Either the killer would turn out to have been magically shielded against identification in some fashion, or they had simply fired from concealment so that the victim never saw his assailant. If Willett had never seen the latter's face, it obviously wouldn't reside in his memories.

She told the driver to pull over at the next pay phone and called Alice Quinn. It would not be strictly accurate to refer to Quinn as a friend, but they had so far managed not to alienate each other during their occasional interactions. Quinn had started as a call girl, now ran a string of high priced temporary companions that had survived the periodic efforts by one faction or another in the city government to put her out of business. She survived where others had fallen because she had insinuated herself into the power structure and knew where both ends of the strings were attached. Quinn was subtle. She never seemed to actually pull any of the strands of her web, but somehow after every wave of political housekeeping it remained intact. Knowledge has a way of conferring immunity.

"Wanda! It's been too long."

"What can I say? My hectic social life doesn't leave much room for old friends."

"So we're old friends now, are we?"

"We are if you can spare me an hour or so."

"Right now?"

"Preferably."

There was a brief hesitation. "All right, come on up. You remember how to find me?"

"As if I could forget."

The cabbie whistled when he heard the address. "Most of the fares I take there are men."

Wanda ignored the curiosity in his voice. "This is business, not pleasure."

"I just drive, lady, I don't judge." But he was smirking.

Quinn's headquarters were discrete. No red lights, no streetwalkers allowed within blocks, a dignified clerk in the lobby to direct traffic. Quinn's business occupied only three floors and she lived in the penthouse but the remaining seven levels were rented out to a variety of businesses and professionals with more socially acceptable lines of endeavor. Wanda gave her name to the clerk, who handed her a gold coin. "This will give you access to the private elevator." She gestured to a shadowy hallway that was marked "Staff Only" and which was probably magically warded. If so, the coin neutralized the barrier.

A few minutes later, she was sitting in Alice Quinn's apartment, drinking a thankfully unflavored brandy. She'd been to the penthouse before but she was still impressed at how subdued her surroundings were. Quinn dressed and lived conservatively. If you had educated eyes, you might notice that she surrounded herself with quality from the hand woven rug underfoot to the cut glass chandelier over the dining room table. But nothing was gaudy or frilly, least of all the woman who lived there.

Quinn was in her late thirties, probably a year or two older than Wanda. She was relaxed and pleasant and didn't ask any questions after ascertaining what her guest wanted to drink. Asking questions made you the supplicant and Quinn always negotiated from a position of power. Wanda took a sip, approved whole heartedly, and decided to come to the point. "How well did you know Nathan Willett?"

Quinn showed no surprise at mention of his name. "The later Mr. Willett was numbered among my acquaintances, but alas not among my friends. He has been a good deal less tolerant of my entrepreneurial efforts than his counterparts on the other papers. His wife may have been a contributing factor. She very publicly refused to shake my hand at some city function a year or two ago. It was supposed to put me in my place, I suppose, but most of the coverage alluded to her ungraciousness."

"Then you won't lament his loss."

"Nor will I celebrate it. He was a relatively minor annoyance. His fulminations may actually have sent some business my way, although I'm sure that's not what he intended. Why are you so interested?"

"His sudden and unexpected death made it impossible for him to attend a meeting with me which he had requested."

"Was he a client?"

"Not yet. We hadn't discussed any specifics."

"I confess to feeling relieved. If he had hired you to find some leverage against me, I'm sure you would have turned up something."

"I'm not sure I would have taken his money if that's what he wanted."

"I wasn't aware that our friendship was so warm." Quinn seemed mildly amused.

Wanda was not there to be amusing. "It's not. I just don't like prudes. So what can you tell me about Willett? I know that he bought his way into the head office at the *Journal*, but I don't know where the money came from."

"His father owned Kobold Mining up in Nome, Alaska. Goblins weren't protected by the minimum wage law or safety regulations in those days so labor was cheap. Just before the mines played out, old Ezra Willett sold off his shares in the company and moved east. About the same time, the goblin hoard in Nome was cleaned out to the last nugget, and rumor had it that Willett was involved in that as well, although no one ever made the charges stick. He bought controlling interest in several local businesses, including the *Journal*, the Tiara Hotel, the Arcanium, and the Unicorn busline. There were some others too."

"He's still alive, isn't he? Retired?"

"Officially, he's retired. In practice, he's still trying to suborn the city government and the Sorcerors' Council. He's made a lot of enemies in both places. I wouldn't have been surprised if Ezra had turned up dead. The son was a relative lightweight."

"Wasn't Ezra involved in some scandal involving the city government?"

"He wasn't used to life in the big city when he first arrived. He tried to buy the mayor's office and the city council; he certainly had enough cash. Made some inroads, but he should have realized he wasn't the only interested party sitting on a pile of gold. When some of his bought and paid for councilors switched sides, he decided to set his sights higher and went after the Sorcerers' Council. He's been waging a kind of guerilla war there ever since but the power balance hasn't shifted significantly these last few years."

"Could the son's death have been a reprisal?"

"Of course it could. It could also be a random mugging. Or maybe someone was offended by one of his editorials. He might even have pissed off his father. Ezra isn't much for sentimentality. Public figures make lots of enemies. Despite my efforts to stay out of the public eye, you'd be amazed how many security spells I subscribe to. And I still had a close call a couple of years back."

"Which of the old man's enemies would be ruthless enough and motivated enough to do something like this?"

Quinn laughed. "It would take less time to list the ones who wouldn't. Top contenders would be Myles Lewis, the deputy mayor, or Audrey Noonan on the city council. Noonan wants to run for the Senate next election and Lewis is supposed to have proposed marriage to some mystery woman. Neither of them wants the applecart bumped let alone upset right now. The sorcerers are harder to judge; they keep things more in the family. I know that Petra Finn hated Willett, but I also heard that Max Taylor wasn't a big fan."

"I don't know that name."

"He calls himself The Whisperer most of the time."

Wanda blinked. "That name I have heard." And not in the most complimentary terms.

"There are more, but if I was making book, those four would have the shortest odds."

Wanda finished her drink and ostentatiously set the glass down and stood up. "Thanks for seeing me, Alice. Do I give this to you?" She held out the enchanted coin.

"The elevator won't work without it. Drop it off at the desk. And don't wait so long to visit. I don't get to make many real friends in my line of work."

"Mine neither."

Wanda wasn't prescient, but as soon as the phone began to ring, she sensed that something was wrong. There were only a handful of people who had her home number, and most of them knew better than to try after midnight. It might have been Bowman calling to let her know how the Crest stakeout had gone, but she was certain that it wouldn't be his voice she heard. There was nothing about the case that couldn't wait until morning, or at least she didn't think there was.

"Coyne here." Her voice sounded too loud. She was swinging her legs over the side of the bed and standing before the caller spoke. She listened calmly, her face blank, and when the message had been delivered she spoke in flat tones. "I'll be right there, Lieutenant." As soon as she heard the dial tone, she called for a cab.

Wanda dressed quickly but methodically, her thoughts racing. It was too soon to speculate but she was clearing her mind of anything that might distract her. When she was dispassionate, she was at the top of her game, and something told her that was where she needed to be. She was standing out front in a light drizzling rain when the cab arrived. The driver recognized her, knew her well enough not to initiate a conversation, and drove her efficiently to the water front. She told him to wait.

There were several muffled voices not far away and dancing spots of light told her which of the piers to approach. A uniformed officer intercepted her a moment later and she identified herself. "Lieutenant Poorhouse called me."

The uniform looked skeptical but nodded. "They're down below. There's a ladder over there. Watch your step."

There were half a dozen figures milling about at the foot of the ladder, but only one of them turned in her direction when she climbed down. "Hello, Wanda. Sorry to get you out in this weather but I knew you'd want to see for yourself."

"Thanks." She moved past him and looked down at the body of Matthew Bowman, who floated face up in the water, one arm half wrapped around a pylon as though he were trying to anchor himself. But it was purely chance because Bowman wouldn't have been trying to do anything after having his heart turned to ash. The gaping hole in his chest looked almost cauterized. "Fire spell?" she asked quietly.

Poorhouse shrugged. "Could be a salamander. The forensic people should be able to tell us something once they've had a look at him."

"Who called it in?"

"Watchman. Saw a flash of light from the other side of the pier. Came over to make sure there wasn't a fire." Poorhouse looked away. "Said he smelled something funny, like burnt meat, so he looked around a little."

"Did he see anything else?"

"A car drove past him but he wasn't paying attention. Dark, an older model, not speeding. Might not be connected. We're still checking for more witnesses but this area is pretty deserted this time of night." He hesitated. "What would Matt have been doing here? Was he working a case?"

It was Wanda's turn to shrug. "He was supposed to be tailing some guy named Lloyd Thursday. I don't know if that would have brought him to the waterfront."

"Why?"

"He was working, Poorhouse. You know I can't say too much. And I don't know a lot myself. Thursday may have been a familiar working with a succubus. That's all I can tell you."

After a pause, Poorhouse nodded. "Do you want to notify his wife or should I?"

Wanda closed her eyes for a second. "I'll do it."

But in the end, she didn't. She couldn't face Ava just then, so instead she called Perry Everdeen and asked him to talk his wife into breaking the news. "Have her tell Ava I'm looking into it and I'll come see her when I know more." Then she dismissed the cabbie with a generous tip she really couldn't afford and walked home. She needed the time to think. The city wasn't actually quiet, even at this time of night, but quiet was a relative value. With the distant traffic noises filtered out, there was little to distract her from her thoughts, and the next hour or so was going to be the only mourning period she allowed herself. Sentiment wouldn't pay the bills or find Bowman's killer. She was actually surprised when she found herself at the apartment building.

CHAPTER TWO

She never made it back to bed. Wanda was half undressed when the door imp opened its eyes and spoke in its usual gravelly voice. "Two unknown men are coming up the stairs."

Wanda sighed and rebuttoned her blouse. She had the door open before her visitors reached the landing. It was Lieutenant Poorhouse and another man she was less happy to recognize. "Hello, Captain. I wasn't expecting you until daylight but I guess you might as well come in. Coffee?"

They waited while she put the pot on but she could feel their eyes on her back.

"How did Mrs. Bowman take the bad news?" asked Captain Dandy.

Wanda shrugged and took down three mugs. None of them matched. She was reluctant to admit her weakness to the two men. "It takes a while to sink in."

"How much do you know about salamanders?"

She turned to face them, leaning back against the narrow counter. The captain was a big man, tall and broad shouldered, with a dark complexion and eyes so inset that they looked like a pair of embedded lenses. "I know what they're capable of and I know they're illegal."

"Would you know how to acquire one?"

"I could find out. But I'm not licensed for paranormal enhancements except what you can buy over the counter. The legit counter. And I don't like paras. Too unpredictable and usually messy. I've never really felt at a disadvantage without them. There's always a price to pay that isn't obvious upfront."

Dandy was unimpressed. "Salamanders generate a powerful aura, you know. It affects everyone around them. Your partner's body practically glowed when the forensic people trained their readers on it. Anyone else who was around would show traces for at least a day or two."

"So why don't you find this Thursday character and check him out?"

The two men exchanged glances. "We're working on it."

Wanda had a good idea where this was going. "In the meantime, you'd like me to come down and submit to an aura reading, right?"

"It might clear you," said Poorhouse hopefully.

"And it might not," added Dandy. "Bowman was past his prime, holding you back. Business hasn't been good lately, not good enough to split anyway."

"Not good enough to kill a man for either. You're wasting time, Captain. Yours and mine."

"Maybe. So how about a quick run down to headquarters for a scan? The night's shot to hell anyway."

"Sure. As soon as you show me the writ."

Dandy frowned. Poorhouse looked unhappy. "Come on, Wanda. It's just a formality. We all want the same thing here. No one thinks you really killed your partner, but we have to eliminate that possibility. You can see that, can't you?"

She gave Dandy a hard look. "Do we really want the same thing? No, I think I'll wait until you convince a judge that there's good enough reason to invade my privacy. Aura readings reveal more than just how recently you've used a salamander to burn a hole through someone. I'm not opening myself up to a fishing expedition without a good reason."

"You're making a mistake," said Dandy coldly. "You don't have a lot of friends in this city, you know."

"So I don't have many to lose either."

"If you won't tell us more about this Thursday character, then what about your client?" Poorhouse was clearly frustrated. "We'll be discreet."

Wanda bit back a tart reply. "I can't tell you that without the client's permission."

"This is a murder case, Coyne." She could see that Dandy had clenched his hands into fists. "That trumps your confidentiality agreement."

"Maybe," she answered quietly. "But I'll still need to talk to my client first. And then maybe my attorney."

Poorhouse shook his head. "Be reasonable, Wanda. We don't have anything to work on. Don't you want us to catch the bastard who did this?"

"I'd rather do it myself, actually." It slipped out. She wondered if she should regret it, but decided she didn't.

Dandy smiled. "I kind of thought you'd say something like that. Maybe you did take care of it yourself."

Wanda kept her face expressionless but felt a surge of tension. She didn't need to be psychic to know that they weren't telling her something that she needed to know. "What's that supposed to mean?"

"It means that Lloyd Thursday is dead. Someone shot him in the back in front of his hotel about an hour ago. No witnesses."

"I don't suppose he was carrying a salamander in his pocket?"

"Funny. You're a very funny person, Coyne. Actually he had a very nice Glock in a shoulder holster and it hadn't been fired recently. So where were you after you left the pier? Don't try to tell us you were consoling the widow because we already checked and you had someone else do it for you. And the door guardian downstairs says you got home just a few minutes before we showed up."

Poorhouse looked uncomfortable. "We checked with the cabbie who drove you over and he says you paid him off at the pier."

Dandy smiled unpleasantly. "Thursday was staying at the Wavefront, about five blocks from where your partner was offed. Easy walking distance. You could've made it there, called him outside, ambushed him, and walked back here without working up a sweat. So did you hire him to kill your partner and then finish him off to close the loop? Or were you just evening the score?"

"How would I know where Thursday was staying?"

"I don't know. You tell us. Maybe your client filled you in."

"Then why would the client hire us to follow him?"

"We only have your word for that so far." Dandy crossed his arms. "Or maybe Bowman tailed him to the Wavefront and then called you with the information before he died."

"You're reaching, Dandy. First you suggest I killed my own partner, then Thursday to avenge my partner. Or maybe I hired Thursday to kill Bowman, and then killed Thursday to cover my tracks. But if that was the case, why did I mention Thursday in the first place?"

"I don't know. You tell us."

Her brain was moving sluggishly. She felt very tired. "How long had Thursday been at the Wavefront?"

"A few days," offered Poorhouse. "So far we haven't found anyone who particularly noticed him. He kept to himself. We might know more tomorrow."

Wanda felt suddenly weary. "I think we're done for the night. Unless you're planning to arrest me."

For the first time, Dandy looked unsure of himself. "Look, Coyne, I'll be square with you. If you did the job, either of them, I'm going to bring you down. I'll feel bad if you were just avenging your partner, but I'll bring you down either way."

"Fair enough. But what if I'm telling the truth?"

"Then you've got nothing to worry about."

They were gone before she realized she had never given them their coffee.

The Boston Herald was lying outside Wanda's door the following morning. Willett's death had made the front page. There was a picture of him and a terse description of his final minutes. He'd left the office at his usual time and had presumably been on his way to the bus terminal when he had been ambushed. He'd been shot from behind four times, three of which would have been fatal. The police hoped to get something from the post mortem scrying but Wanda knew it was unlikely and the story implied the same. It looked on the face of it like a random killing, except that no one had robbed the corpse. The story speculated that Willett had, like most people in the news business, accumulated a corps of enemies, but they tactfully named no names. Wanda watched the television news, which mentioned that Willett's sometimes overbearing moral stance had caused tension between himself and his father, but there was no attempt to develop the theme.

She decided to pay her respects to Willett's widow before going to the office and hailed a cab, but when she got there a dark colored limousine was pulling up in front of the house. Wanda told the driver to pull over a block short and idle for a minute, during which time a tall man in a theatrically long black cloak got out of the limousine and walked to the front door. Wanda didn't see the visitor's face but she didn't have to. This was the Whisperer, whose membership in the Sorcerers' Council had been and still was controversial given their efforts to promote transparency and allay public fears about the magically endowed.

"I changed my mind. Take me downtown."

When Wanda arrived at her office, Perry Everdeen glanced nervously at the inner office door. "She's in there, waiting."

Wanda rolled her eyes. "Couldn't you have told her I wasn't coming in today?"

Perry shrugged. "She caught me off guard. And for all I knew, you were expecting her."

"Yeah, right." Wanda drew a deep breath and opened the door.

Ava was a short, heavy set woman who affected a hairstyle and mode of dress much too young for her years. She rose from where she sat and hugged Wanda tightly. "Who could have done this, Wanda, and why?" Her expression shouted grief but her voice was heavily laden with indifference.

"I don't know yet, Ava." Wanda managed to disengage. "But I'm going to find out. Have you told his brother yet?"

Ava, dry eyed, sniffed and half turned away. It was no secret that she and Matthew had barely spoken to one another of late, had effectively stopped being man and wife more than ten years earlier. "I called him this morning. He's flying in later today."

"He's a good man. He'll take care of things for you."

"Wanda, I have to ask you something. Please don't take offense. It wasn't you, was it?"

For a few seconds, Wanda couldn't process the question. "Of course not. What would make you think such a thing?"

"Matthew could be very difficult, and I know that things weren't going well. We've been nibbling away at our savings for the last three years and I suppose you must be heavily in debt. The insurance money all goes to me but you get his share of the agency. I wouldn't even blame you particularly. Matthew hasn't carried his weight in a long time."

Wanda shook her head, unable to think of an appropriate response. "I think you should go home, Ava. This has all been a great shock and you're not thinking clearly."

Ava Bowman seemed to want to say something more, but then she got a knowing look on her face and nodded. "All right. I understand. I shouldn't have said anything this soon." She stood up and shouldered her bag. "I'll be in touch." And she left.

Wanda shook her head and sat down behind her desk. Did everyone think she had killed her partner? Did she really seem capable of such a thing? She wasn't surprised or offended by Captain Dandy's suspicions. She understood his mindset. Ava Bowman wasn't a particularly intelligent or perceptive woman, but she should have known better.

Perry Everdeen stuck his head through the door. "How'd it go?"

Wanda spread her hands expressively. "She thinks I killed Matthew."

Perry came all the way into the room. "Why would you do that?"

"Apparently I'm obsessed with being sole proprietor of this very lucrative business." She glanced around to indicate the shabby room with its shabby furniture.

"She's not very practical, is she?"

"The police think I killed Lloyd Thursday."

Perry eased into the seat opposite her. "Who's he?"

"The man Matthew was supposed to be following last night after he met with our new client, Miss Crest."

"For what it's worth, I don't think you killed anyone. You didn't, did you?"

"Not recently, no. But that may change soon."

"I had a thought, but it's evil."

"All of my thoughts tend toward the dark side lately. Shoot."

"Could Ava have knocked off her husband? They weren't on good terms and I know he was well insured."

"I can't quite see Ava stalking her husband along a pier in the middle of the night with a hooded basilisk clutched in her hot little hands."

"Not even if I told you that she'd just gotten home herself when Julia and I showed up last night to tell her Matthew was dead? She looked surprised, but she could have faked it. And she sure wasn't heartbroken."

"No surprise about the latter. I never understood why Matthew stayed with her. Misplaced loyalty, I suppose."

"It was more like an armistice than a marriage."

"How could you tell she'd been out?"

"I couldn't, actually, but Julia knew right away. Ava was still dressed when we arrived and I figured she was just a night owl. But Julia told me that no woman would sit around the house in such uncomfortable shoes, that she must have been out until just before we arrived. She'd also been drinking; we had to tell her Matt was dead twice before it sank in."

"Interesting. But maybe she was just back from a tryst with her lover."

Perry made a face. "She's past that, I think."

Wanda sighed. "You're so young. We're never past that; we just get less selective." Perry started for the door and Wanda had a thought. "Can you get me a number for Ezra Willett?"

"The same Ezra Willett who owns half of the city?"

"More like ten percent, but yes, that's the one."

"It's probably unlisted."

"I have confidence in you."

It took ten minutes.

She was connected to a young man who claimed to be Ezra Willett's administrative assistant, but who didn't think he could arrange an appointment. "I'm afraid Mr. Willett has a very tight schedule and there has recently been a tragedy in the family as well. Perhaps I could help you?" The tragedy seemed to be an afterthought.

"No, I'm afraid not. I just happened to have some information about his son's death that I thought he might want to know, but I guess I can just talk to someone over at the *Herald* instead."

There was a profound silence. "If you can hold on for a moment, Miss Coyne, I'll see if something can be managed."

Wanda sat back and automatically reached for the cigarettes she'd given up six months earlier. The voice returned more quickly than she expected. "As it happens, Mr. Willett has cancelled his other appointments today out of respect for his son. Could you call this morning?"

"Half an hour." Wanda hung up, letting her thoughts churn for a few minutes, then made another call and set up a lunch date. Satisfied, she rose from her chair and walked through the door. "I'll be back after lunch, Perry. If you run out of space for all our prospective clients you can ask them to line up in the hall." Marvella

Crest had been their first paying client in two weeks. Nathan Willett might have been the second, except that he had no further need for their services.

"I'll try to keep the crowd under control," said Perry.

CHAPTER THREE

Ezra Willett lived in a Victorian brownstone in Back Bay. He also owned the two adjacent houses which were empty when they weren't being used for guests. He had purchased them as a buffer between himself and his neighbors. The door guardian was so powerful that Wanda could actually feel it touch her mind, searching for any hint of hostile intent, and there was an armed guard stationed in the front hall. The windows all had that faint suggestion of fuzziness that suggested avoidance spells. Would be burglars would become thoroughly nauseated if they didn't have the right countercharm.

An attendant, female, remotely pretty in a severe sort of way, led Wanda to a small room lined with books that probably had never been read. She didn't offer Wanda a drink, not even coffee, and if she had smiled her lower jaw might have shattered. She was still in the room when a much older man entered, balding but with a circle of white hair around his temples, and almost unnaturally thick eyebrows. He glowered at her for a second and glanced at the secretary, who almost ran out of the door.

"What is this all about, Miss Coyne? Time is valuable to me even at my age. Especially at my age."

Wanda waited just long enough to prove that it was deliberate before answering. "I'm a private investigator. Two days ago your son called our office and set up an appointment. He was rather secretive about the reason for his call, insisted that he couldn't be seen consulting a detective, and invited me to have dinner at his house last night. And then he was dead."

"My son was editor of a newspaper. He was always investigating something or another. Some people prefer not to be subjected to public scrutiny."

Wanda nodded. "Your son has a staff of well paid, very competent investigative reporters who presumably will continue at their job despite the change at the top. Some of them are excellent at their job. Why would he need my services?"

"Maybe he had too many irons in the fire, or maybe there was some reason he needed a fresh face. Most of his people are pretty well known."

"I think he may have been killed to prevent him from talking to me."

Willett considered her words without changing expression. "The police might be interested in your story, but it doesn't strike me as very helpful unless you knew something about why he wanted to see you."

"I have no idea. He was very terse when he called to set things up."

"Then might I ask what your purpose is in coming to see me? I don't see that either of us can help the other."

"I was at your son's house last night when his wife received a telephone call that distressed her considerably."

For the first time there was emotion in Willett's voice. "That worthless bitch! I told him that it was a mistake marrying her. She changed him. I assume you noticed the kind of woman she is."

Wanda ignored the enticement to comment. "I believe that the call was to tell her he was dead, and that was before the body was officially discovered. The only person I can think of who would have been in a position to make that call is the killer, or whoever was behind the killer."

Ezra's eyes flashed. There was anger there, but something else as well. Something Wanda couldn't identify.

"It wouldn't surprise me if she had taken out a contract on him. No, that's not fair. He could never have measured up to her impossibly pure standards, but she liked having an influential husband. Have you told the police about this yet?"

"No."

"Then you ought to. They'll lock her away someplace too strict even for her taste." Willett seemed pleased by the prospect.

Wanda shook her head. "Not without evidence. She'll deny that the call ever happened, or say that it was later than it actually was. If I go to the cops with what I've got, they'll either pat me on the head and file it away under useless or decide I'm trying to work up some publicity for my agency."

"The authorities are sometimes skeptical of even the most innocent of motives." He had reverted to being detached.

"Is there any reason to think she might have wanted him dead?"

Willett turned away and began packing. "No one could have measured up to her impossible standards, but he tried. On one occasion, I suggested that he take a mistress to relieve the pressure and he almost had a stroke, insisted that he loved her beyond anything in the world, all that romantic crap. I doubt that she actually liked or even approved of him, but even I don't think their relationship had deteriorated quite that far. On the other hand I've seen very little of either of them these past few years."

"Not a particularly close family, I gather."

"What business is it of yours?" Willett's face suddenly flushed. "All you've done, Miss Coyne, is tell me what you can't do. If that's what you came here for, then you're wasting my time. And probably your own as well."

Wanda ignored him and remained seated. "I decided to pay a visit to your daughter-in-law today, to express my sympathies. But I didn't go in because she already had company. An old friend of yours, in fact. The Whisperer."

She could almost hear the wheels turning in the old man's head. "Now that is the most interesting thing you've said since you've been here. My son did not care for Mr. Taylor at all. He believed that the Whisperer, and most of the other Council members, utilized their position and powers outside of the guidelines under which the use of advanced magic is supposedly governed. But Mr. Taylor has other attributes which endeared him to Gladys though not to my son."

"You don't think they were having an affair then?"

Willett laughed. "No, I'm quite certain that they were not involved sexually. It wouldn't have appealed to either of them." He laughed again, but Wanda didn't get the joke.

"Perhaps he was merely offering his condolences then."

Willett frowned at her. "You don't believe that any more than I do. There's something fishy going on. Taylor prefers to stay out of the limelight. Even a passing connection to a murder case would put him off."

Wanda decided to shift to another line of inquiry. "You and your son had not been on good terms for some time, I take it."

Willett looked uncomfortable. "We were not temperamentally suited to enjoy one another's company, but we had a positive business relationship or I would not have signed over the *Journal* to him."

"There were rumors that there were strings attached."

"There are always such rumors. I admit that I sometimes suggested areas of investigation and Nathan generally followed up. But they were valid news stories and Nathan had ethics – more than I frankly – and refused to do a hatchet job unless it was justified by the facts."

"He still managed to make a lot of enemies."

"Everyone who is successful makes a lot of enemies. I asked a few questions about you after your call. You are not in the running for citizen of the year either."

"I have my share of detractors. I'm rather proud of most of them."

"Let's hope that you don't add me to that roster." He smiled but there was a hint of iron in his voice.

Wanda smiled back. "I think we'd both be better off if we remain cordial. In fact, I'd better be off myself before I overstay my welcome." She stood up. "Thank you for agreeing to see me."

"I assume you will pass along what you know to the police. If Gladys and her shadowy friend killed my son, I want them punished."

"It sounds to me like you want them punished even if they didn't do it."

"You're an impertinent woman." He sighed. "But a perceptive one. I have my reasons for disliking them both."

"I've been told that before and I confess neither of them is on my Christmas card list either. I'll leave you my card." She set one down on the end table. "If you think of something that might throw light on the subject, I'll be happy to hear of it."

"What's in this for you? No one is paying you to find out the truth."

"Let's just say I frown on people killing potential clients before they can give me a retainer. It sets a bad precedent."

He arched an eyebrow. "What if I decided to provide that retainer?"

"I would respectfully decline. I prefer not to deal with clients who won't tell me the truth." Then she laughed. "Unfortunately, most of them don't."

CHAPTER FOUR

A half hour later, Wanda stepped out of a cab and walked around the downtown for several minutes before feeling reasonably certain that she wasn't being tailed. Captain Dandy was a relatively honest cop but he didn't like her and he'd love to have a legitimate reason to take her license. She hailed another cab and had this one drop her off two blocks from the Golden Dawn Hotel. After another brief circumlocution to throw off anyone who might still somehow be following her, she slipped into the lobby and approached the desk clerk. The first news she received did not please her.

"Miss Crest checked out this morning. You just missed her."

"Did she leave any messages?"

Of course not.

She thanked the clerk. "Is Bob Fetter around today?"

An eyebrow went up. "He should be in his office."

She thanked him again and made her way to the back of the lobby where a service corridor led to a door marked Security. Her knock got an immediate response and she went inside.

Fetter rose from his desk smiling broadly. He was a big man, both tall and heavily built, and while there were signs that he was softening around the edges, the core remained firm. "Wanda. It's good to see you. Sit yourself down. I just heard about Matthew. Terrible thing. Do they have any idea who did it?"

"At the moment, I seem to head the list of suspects."

"That's crazy."

"It's all crazy."

He nodded briefly in sympathy. "Did you know Matthew was here last night?"

"I did, actually. He was on a stakeout."

Fetter nodded. "I thought as much. He was in the lobby gift shop looking at charm bracelets and I knew that wasn't his kind of thing so it had to be a job. I was going to say hello but decided to steer clear just in case. You don't think it was one of our guests who killed him, do you?"

"It's too soon to think anything just yet. I do have a question about one of your guests though, a Miss Marvella Crest. She checked out this morning."

"What can I tell you?"

"Anything you've got."

Fetter swiveled his chair to one side and whisked a velvet cloth off a large crystal ball. His mouth moved slightly as he sub vocalized his commands and his eyes glazed as he stared into the prismatic depths. Wanda settled back into her seat and waited patiently until the brief trance ended and Fetter turned back to her.

"She checked in a week ago today. One bag. Paid with cash. There were no calls from her room phone and no known visitors. Maid service reports nothing unusual in the room. Checked out this morning, still by herself. She told the clerk she had a cab waiting but no one saw what company it was from. No forwarding address."

"Doesn't help much."

"Sorry."

"Not your fault. Thanks for trying."

Perry was looking unhappy when Wanda arrived back at the office. "Captain Dandy was here."

"Glad I missed him."

"He wasn't looking for you. He wanted to ask me some questions."

"Let me guess. Had Matthew and I been arguing? How are out finances? Are we paying our bills? Have there been any violent arguments? Do you know anything about Lloyd Thursday or our as yet unidentified client?"

Perry nodded. "He also wanted to know what kind of guns you owned."

"Did you tell him?"

"I told him about the ones you have registered."

"Smart man."

"And Miss Crest called." His voice had softened.

Wanda raised an eyebrow. "Did she now?"

"She wants to meet with you."

"The feeling is mutual. Where and when?"

"As soon as possible. She's staying at the Tiara and she said she'd be in all day. But she's registered under an assumed name, so you should ask for Miss White's room."

Wanda glanced at her watch. "I have a luncheon date first. If she calls back, tell her to expect me about 1:30."

Sharon Llewellyn was not happy to discover that Wanda was a private investigator. "I thought you said this was about a job."

"It is. I never said it was about your job." Llewellyn was, or had been, private secretary to Nathan Willett. She was strikingly attractive and Wanda wondered idly if the possessive Mrs. Nathan Willett had been entirely pleased by the personnel arrangements at her husband's place of business. On the other hand, Miss Llewellyn was sporting a very ostentatious engagement ring so maybe that ameliorated her appearance to some degree. Wanda had never really understood the jealousy thing. It defied rational analysis.

"I should walk out right now." But Llewellyn made no move to rise. "I almost didn't come in the first place. I'm getting married in the fall and I imagine my husband will prefer that I manage things at home." She moved her hand deliberately to draw attention to the diamond. "We certainly won't need the money."

"Congratulations. Look, I just want to ask a few questions. At worst you get a free lunch."

"And at best?"

"Ezra Willett is aware of my interest in his son's death. He would almost certainly wish to reward anyone who helped advance my investigation if it proves successful in finding out who the killer is. No matter how well off your fiancé is, it never hurts to have a little mad money hidden away that he doesn't know about." She ventured a conspiratorial wink, knowing it wouldn't be very convincing. But then again, Llewellyn didn't require that much persuasion.

"Well, alright, I guess. But I don't know anything about it. The murder, I mean." The waiter took their orders. Llewellyn might be skinny but she apparently had a healthy appetite. Or a particularly effective and expensive body management spell. "You're working for Mr. Willett then? The older one I mean."

Wanda parried. "Our relationship is informal for the moment. There are reasons why it's best if a formal arrangement awaits developments."

"Of course," said Llewellyn, as if she knew what that meant. Since Wanda didn't know herself, that was unlikely.

"I gather father and son didn't get along all that well."

"Well, they disagreed a lot, but I don't think they were all that different about what they wanted. Mr. Willett, my Mr. Willett that is, was more concerned with methods. He told me once that his father had never accepted that times changed and the old way of doing things wasn't appropriate anymore." Their food arrived and she assaulted it as though it had personally wronged her.

"Do you think Nathan was worried that his reporters might find something that implicated his father?"

Her mouth was full but Llewellyn nodded, then swallowed. "He tried to stay away from that part of things because he didn't want to know anything that might reflect badly on the old man. But Mr. Willett, the older one, has his fingers in so many pies that it's hard to turn over a rock and not find his fingerprints."

Wanda wrestled with that mixed metaphor while she ate some of her Pad Thai. "Did anything out of the ordinary happen in the last couple of days?"

"Not that I know of, but I only knew bits and pieces of what was going on. You know, being his secretary and all, I overheard things I probably wasn't meant to. But I wasn't his confidant. He played his cards close to his chest and kept his right hand from knowing what the left was doing."

Wanda tried to distill meaning from the clichés. "There wasn't any kind of task force at the paper? No inner circle? Something that wouldn't be known to the staff at large."

Llewellyn shook her head. "He dealt with each reporter separately most of the time. And he almost never had me in to take notes."

"But he had files?"

"There's nothing important in them. He didn't even keep them locked."

"So what did he do yesterday afternoon?"

Llewellyn paused with her fork half raised. Her plate was already nearly empty. "He met with the advertising department right after lunch. Our revenues have been slipping and he wasn't happy about it. Then there was a technical meeting about some upgrades to the press equipment. That seemed to go on forever. He was technically free after that, One of our distributors stopped in but it was just a social call and she didn't stay long. That covers most of the afternoon."

"And he never left his office?"

"No. Oh wait, he did go out for about half an hour between the two long meetings. He said he was out of cigarettes and I offered to go for him but he said he wanted to stretch his legs."

"Where would he have gone?"

"He didn't say, but there's a smokeshop in the lobby of our building."

"That wouldn't have taken half an hour."

"No, but like he said, he wanted to stretch his legs. Oh, and I think there was a letter he said he was going to drop in the mail."

"A letter? Who was it for?"

"I don't know. I didn't type it for him and he didn't show it to me. But he had accounting write up a check just before that and the check wasn't on his desk later, so he probably mailed a payment to someone."

"How much was the check?"

She looked uncomfortable. "I wasn't really supposed to see it. They delivered it in an envelope. But it wasn't sealed and it slipped out." She was lying about that, but Wanda didn't care. "It was for ten thousand dollars."

"Who was it made out to?"

"Diana Marks."

"Who is she?"

"I have no idea. I've never heard the name before."

Lunch took longer than Wanda had expected because Llewellyn wanted dessert. Wanda called the office and asked Perry to find out what he could about Diana Marks.

CHAPTER FIVE

Marvella Crest, now Esther White, did not look happy to see Wanda, which was strange since she had requested the meeting. She glanced along the corridor as though to ensure that her visitor was alone before ushering her into the room. A small suitcase was lying on the bed, open but only half empty. What Wanda could see looked look good quality, pricey but not exorbitant.

"I imagine you want to ask me some questions." Crest sounded resentful.

"Considering that my partner was found floating in the harbor last night with a hole burned through his chest and that your Mr. Thursday was shot dead in the street a short time later, and in view of the fact that the police seem to think I'm probably responsible for one or the other or both, then yes, I do have some questions."

"Well, let me save you some time. I'm sorry but everything I told you the other day was a lie."

"We knew there was something fishy about it at the time. If you're going to play the naïve country bumpkin, you need a cheaper wardrobe."

She looked surprised. "If you thought I was lying, then why did you take my case?"

"Actually we were more interested in taking your money. You did give us a retainer, remember? But that doesn't mean we weren't suspicious, Miss… What is your name anyway? Your real name?"

"Bridges. Faye Bridges." She made it sound like the truth but Wanda still had her suspicions.

"So what's the real story, Miss Bridges?"

The younger woman clasped her hands together and turned away. "I have to ask you something first. Am I responsible for Mr. Bowman's death?"

"Well, you did say that Mr. Thursday seemed like a dangerous man, so we were warned. If he killed my partner, that is. I'm still not clear about that. And if he did, why was he shot multiple times in the back?"

"Did he have a family? Your partner, I mean."

Wanda thought about it. "No, not really."

"At least there's that."

"The police are very curious about you."

"What have you told them?"

"Nothing yet. Client confidentiality, remember? But this is a murder and they'll keep at it until they find something whether I tell them or not. And if it means finding Matthew's killer, then I'll be inclined to cooperate. So you need to give me a good reason why I should keep your name – or names – out of this."

"You don't think I had anything to do with the killings, do you?"

"I don't know. Did you?"

Bridges looked shocked. "How could you think such a thing?"

"I can think it because I don't know much about you, and what I do know about you turns out to be mostly lies. So how much can I assume is true?"

"I deserve that." She looked abashed, but not overly so.

"Yes, you do. But that doesn't solve our problem."

"I've made some mistakes, done some things that I shouldn't have, but I'm not really a bad person, Miss Coyne. Really. And I've trusted the wrong people, like Lloyd Thursday, and that makes it hard for me to trust anyone else. Surely you can understand that?"

They were still both standing, but Wanda looked around and settled into a plush chair before answering. "You might as well drop the act. You're good, I grant you, but only for one performance. The sad little girl in over her head bit works best with guys and I imagine that's where you direct most of your efforts. Women much less perceptive than I am would see right through it. You're hardly the helpless lamb in a world of wolves."

Bridges stood rigid, her face coloring, but there was a flash of anger and perhaps just a hint of fear in her eyes. "You can't condemn me for resorting to what's worked in the past."

Wanda reserved judgment on that one. "So how about telling me the truth."

Bridges began to pace and no longer met Wanda's eyes, which was not a good sign. "I can't blame you for not trusting me. I wouldn't if our situations were reversed." Her voice was more confident than it had been. "I don't imagine you'll believe me but I hated having to lie to you and your partner."

"And you're going to tell me the truth now."

"Yes. I'll tell you anything you want to know."

Wanda didn't believe her, but there was no way to change the situation at the moment. "You can start by telling me what happened last night."

"Lloyd met me in the restaurant like we'd arranged. I didn't see Mr. Bowman at all, but when we were done and Lloyd was leaving, he was standing there in the lobby. I asked Lloyd for a cigarette so that I was sure he'd see us together and then I went up to my room."

"And what did you do then?"

"Nothing. I sat up for a while because I couldn't sleep. I tried reading a novel but I couldn't concentrate, so I finally went to bed. Then I saw the papers this morning and I panicked and checked out of the hotel and came here. I couldn't think of anything else to do so I called your office and I've been here ever since."

"So you were aware before I got here that Thursday and Matthew were both dead."

"Yes."

"But if Thursday was the only person who knew where you were staying, there was no reason to switch hotels after he was dead."

Bridges jerked as though she'd touched a live wire, tried unsuccessfully to cover up. "All right, I had another reason. Someone searched my room at the Golden Dawn."

Wanda frowned. "That's very hard to believe. They have first rate warding devices. The security people would have known right away if there'd been a breach." Wanda knew this wasn't strictly true. For a variety of reasons, door guardians were impractical for public places, so hotels generally used a security spell that sensed forced entry – broken windows, picked locks. But someone equipped with a universal master key could open any lock without triggering any but the most sophisticated and expensive protective magic. Alternatively one could steal a key from one of the staff, or bribe one for that matter.

"Well someone must have found a way around them because my clothes were rearranged."

"Maybe the maid tidied up."

"This was more than that. Someone was looking for something."

"Like what?"

"I have no idea." This was clearly a lie.

"What time did this happen?"

The younger woman bit her lip. "I'm not sure, but probably while I was at your office yesterday. I stayed close to the hotel otherwise in case Lloyd tried to get in touch with me."

"And you're not going to tell me what this mysterious visitor was looking for?"

"I've told you all that I can."

"Why don't you tell me why I'm here? You didn't ask me over just to confess, and obviously I can't follow Lloyd Thursday for you. So just what is it that you want me to do?"

"I want you to keep the police away from me."

"In order to do that, I'll have to find out who killed Matthew and Thursday. Assuming it wasn't you."

"It wasn't, but I understand what you're saying."

"Let's start with Thursday. What do you know about him? The truth this time."

Bridges sighed and finally stopped pacing and sat down on the end of the bed. "We met in Tokyo, at the Mizuchi exposition. You know, the water dragons."

"Go on."

"He was supposed to help me. I was paying him a retainer. But he was playing both sides of the game."

"What game?"

"I can't tell you that."

Wanda made an impatient sound. "We're not going to get far this way. Why did you hire us to follow him?"

"I wanted to confirm what I already suspected. If he met with...my enemies...then I'd know I couldn't trust him anymore."

"Do you think he killed my partner?"

"He must have. Who else is there?"

"Would Thursday be familiar with arcane weaponry? Matthew was killed by a salamander."

Bridges threw her head back. "Then he must have. I didn't know everything about the man. He could have been an archmage for all I knew."

"Salamanders are very awkward to deal with. They're too bulky to keep in a pocket and too recognizable to carry around openly. And Thursday had a very serviceable firearm that would have been quicker, simpler, and just as deadly."

"I don't know. Lloyd did have a flare for the dramatic at times."

"There's been entirely too much drama in this case already."

"That's not my fault."

"Maybe not." Wanda mulled things over for a few seconds. "Just how tight a corner have you gotten yourself into?"

"Pretty tight."

"What are the chances that someone with a salamander might come looking for you next?"

"It's possible. Likely, actually. Not necessarily with a salamander, of course. Can you help me?"

"You could go to the police."

"No," she said firmly. "I can't do that."

"I can't perform miracles. Hell, I can't even perform incantations. You'd be better off with an agency that uses paranormals."

"I feel safer with you."

Wanda was not flattered. "So who had reason to kill Thursday? Maybe he hadn't sold out after all and your enemies took him out of the picture. Or maybe he had enemies of his own."

"I don't know. If I did, I'd tell you."

"Would you? You haven't told me much of anything else. What did you want him to do for you? Why are you really here in Boston?"

Bridges didn't answer, just shook her head. Frustrated, Wanda stood up and started toward the door.

"Do you even have a brother?"

"No. You won't tell the police, will you?" Bridges was also standing.

"No, not for the time being. But it's very hard to do a job when your employer won't even tell you exactly what it is that she wants you to do. And don't tell me that you're sorry again." Bridges looked suitably cowed. "I'll be in touch." Wanda let herself out.

Wanda returned to her office and found Perry looking as though he would burst if he didn't tell her what he'd found out. She held up a hand for silence and poured herself a cup of coffee, then sat down on one of the visitor's chairs. "Okay, what have you got?"

"Diana Marks is, or at least was, a high priced call girl. She worked for Alice Quinn for a couple of years and there were rumors that she was tight with the boss. Then something happened, details unknown, and they had a falling out. Marks went off and freelanced for a while, made an abortive effort to run her own string of ladies. There was more friction and it looked like it might get ugly but then Marks got herself a high profile boyfriend who apparently wanted an exclusive arrangement. She rolled up the business and has been off the market ever since."

"Who was the boyfriend?"

"That's where it gets interesting. His name is Max Taylor."

Wanda whistled. "The Whisperer. That's an interesting coincidence."

"You don't like coincidences."

"Yeah, I know, but thanks for reminding me."

"And you won't like the next one either. They're still a happy couple as far as anyone knows, but they keep separate apartments."

"Sorcerers are like that. They don't like having anyone too close."

"Sounds lonely. Anyway, I found out where Marks is living now and it's only two blocks away from where Willett got himself killed in an alley."

"Great work. I'd give you a bonus if I could afford to give you a bonus."

"I wouldn't know what to do with it anyway. I've gotten so used to living on bread and water that meat and vegetables don't taste right anymore."

"I told you when you took the job that it would change your life."

Wanda took her coffee into the inner office and called her lawyer, who refused to commit himself about how far she could go pleading client confidentiality in a murder case. "Do what you want for now, but you might have to surrender your client's name later on. I'll look into it, but the law doesn't give you a lot of leeway when there's a capital crime involved."

"Can the cops use a diviner to find out without my help?"

"Astral searches are pretty rare. They'd have to present an awfully good case to a judge or compelling evidence that your withholding of that information put innocent lives at risk."

She had barely hung up the phone when Perry came through the door and closed it behind him. "There's someone here to see you."

"I hope it's a client."

"Maybe. There's something odd about this one. I get bad vibes."

"Since when were you fey?"

"Since this guy walked in."

"Has he got a name?"

"Joe Muscat."

Wanda shook her head. "Rings no bells. Send him in."

CHAPTER SIX

Muscat was around thirty years old, short, with spiky black hair that was barely visible under a red fez. It was a cool day but he was visibly sweating. He seemed very ill at ease and half turned back to the door before advancing toward the desk. His eyes kept darting around the room as though he expected to catch someone spying on him. Wanda offered him a seat, which he accepted readily enough, but he seemed reluctant to speak. She took an instant dislike to him and tried to decide whether it was more advantageous to prod him or wait him out, but her own impatience won.

"What can I do for you, Mr. Muscat?"

"I read about your troubles in today's paper, Miss Coyne. May I offer my condolences?"

"If you wish, but I hardly think you came here today just to say how sorry you felt that my partner, whom I assume you've never met, has passed on."

"No, of course not."

"Then what does bring you to my office?" She allowed him to hear a hint of asperity.

"I also read of another unfortunate affair involving a Mr. Thursday."

"I read that as well. I didn't know the gentleman."

"Still, it does seem coincidental that both men died violently within hours of one another, their deaths separated by only a short distance."

"There are dozens of murders in this city every year, Mr. Muscat. The odds are that sometimes they will occur close together in time as well as space."

"Then you don't believe there is any connection between the two incidents?"

"I didn't say that. I prefer to keep an open mind in situations like this. Do you have reason to believe that they are related?"

"I am not certain, but I was aware of the existence of Mr. Thursday and I had some personal interest in the man. There is an article missing, the personal property of my employer, which I had hoped Mr. Thursday might enable me to recover."

"Mr. Thursday was not one of my clients, Mr. Muscat. As I mentioned, I had never even met the gentleman."

"No, but perhaps you knew of him. Pardon my bluntness, Miss Coyne, but this is a matter of considerable importance. I would be willing to pay a substantial reward to anyone who could assist me."

"What exactly is this property?"

"It's a gargoyle. Not a live one, but a statue. A deceptively plain looking item with considerable historical and sentimental value. It was stolen from my employer some time ago and he is determined to recover his property."

"The police haven't been able to help you?"

Muscat looked even more uncomfortable than previously, which Coyne would have thought impossible until she saw it. "The authorities are not aware of the theft. I trust your discretion in telling you this, but my employer's title to the statue is rather dubious. As you must know, there are laws restricting the export of certain historical artifacts. In this case, unofficial fees were paid to expedite the process outside of normal channels. I assure you that the moral ownership of the statue is not in question, only its presence in this country."

"I understand."

"The reward would be ten thousand dollars, payable in cash, immediately upon receipt of the gargoyle. I have it with me now." He patted his pocket.

Wanda whistled. "I'm impressed. I wish I had what you're looking for, but unfortunately I don't. If you would like to leave a retainer and provide me with some more information, I might be able to look further into the matter."

Muscat sighed. "I had hoped that we could avoid any unpleasantness but I see that it must be otherwise." He stood up suddenly, reached into his pocket, and took out not a wad of money but what looked like a piece of ivory, then extended his arm toward Wanda. "I'm sure you recognize what this is. You will please stand and place your hands against the wall."

Wanda's pulse quickened but she gave no outward sign that she was affected at all by the clear threat. "You are aware that possession of a dragon's tooth is against the law in this state, aren't you?" It was one of the few weapons that could be brought undetected through all but the most stringent security spells.

"Save the banter and do as you're told. I'm going to search your office, and I would prefer not to kill you in order to do so, but it's a preference not an imperative."

"Be my guest. We might save some time if you told me what you're looking for."

Muscat ignored the implied question. "I must insist that you follow my instructions promptly." He waved the dragon tooth expressively.

Wanda slowly rose from her seat and stepped back from the desk, but she didn't turn away from Muscat. Her troublesome guest was clearly ill at ease but she was pretty sure he meant what he said. "You do remember that Perry is just outside, don't you? I wouldn't want him to walk in on us and spoil your plans." Or get himself killed.

"Don't be concerned about the young man. I placed a locking spell on the door. We should be undisturbed for another hour or until I lift it."

Wanda gave a mock whistle. "That means you're either a reasonably competent mage or you can afford to buy some expensive equipment. Which is it?"

"My resources are none of your concern. Please place your hands on the wall. I need to ascertain that you have no weapons on your person."

Wanda raised her hands but made no move to turn away. Muscat looked as though he was going to say something but thought better of it. With the dragon tooth extended, he came close enough that she could smell his cologne, but he stayed just out of reach. "If you're going to pat me down, I hope you'll be a proper gentleman."

Muscat smirked. "There is no necessity for physical contact. We are close enough. Please stay where you are."

His free hand slipped into a pocket and eased out an ornate amulet on a silver chain. It looked and probably was very old and the chain snagged. Involuntarily Muscat glanced down toward the problem and as he did so Wanda lunged forward and brought the edge of her hand down on his wrist. The dragon tooth slipped from his fingers and fell to the carpet, but by then she was turning and driving an elbow into Muscat's ribs. He staggered back a step, tripped over his own feet, and fell awkwardly. Wanda stooped and picked up the dragon tooth, placed it in the drawer of her desk while Muscat was rising to his hands and knees.

She reached down and pulled Muscat half erect, then made a fist of her free hand. He never saw it coming. The blow caught him on the point of his chin and his head snapped back, his eyes wide with surprise. He was unconscious before he hit the floor this time.

Methodically she went through the unconscious man's capacious pockets. She removed the amulet, which bore an inscription she couldn't read, a few coins, one of which had Greek characters, his wallet and handkerchief, a set of keys, a small ivory case – empty – which was just the right size to hold the dragon tooth, a fountain pen, a miniature scroll inscribed with unfamiliar characters, and a brass charm in the shape of a padlock. The wallet contained identification cards in the name of Joseph Muscat, so he either was who he claimed to be or he'd had forgeries made, a fair amount of cash, a few credit cards, and a ticket to the that evening's performance at the Arcanium. Muscat also wore a wristwatch, a newer model that automatically adjusted when its bearer passed between time zones. The fountain pen seemed to be exactly that.

Muscat was still unconscious when she finished examining his property and replaced it pretty much where she'd found it, so she seated herself and waited. Eventually he groaned and stirred a little, but a few more minutes passed before he ventured to stand up. He seemed surprised to see Wanda watching him so calmly, but didn't speak until he had staggered over to the chair, rubbing his sore chin, and dropped into it.

"I wouldn't really have killed you," he said at last, not meeting her eyes. "It's no longer lethal."

"I knew that. Dragon teeth lose their sheen when they've been discharged. This one was dull with age."

"But you struck me anyway. You could simply have refused to cooperate."

She nodded. "Possibly I was just expressing disappointment. You did dangle a mythical ten thousand dollars in front of me and then snatch it away."

Muscat shook his head vigorously. "I was sincere in my offer and it still stands. Give me the gargoyle and I will pay you as stipulated." He glanced around the office. "If it is here, I can call and have a courier bring the cash immediately."

"It's a very tempting offer. Or it would be tempting if I had the gargoyle."

Muscat was clearly dismayed by this information. "But if you don't have it, why didn't you let me search your office? Why risk a physical confrontation?"

"I'm a very private person. But I'm also very curious. Just who is this mysterious employer of yours?"

Muscat shook his head. "I cannot divulge that information. He is a wealthy man whom it is unwise to thwart and I am his confidential agent. That is all you need to know."

"What I need to know and what I want to know are two separate categories, Mr. Muscat. It would be to your benefit to cooperate with me. Two men have died, you'll recall, and this little interview tells me that you're tied into last night's activities. I imagine the police would be very interested in talking to you."

Somewhat recovered, Muscat allowed himself to relax slightly. "I doubt that you will pursue that particular course, Miss Coyne. The trust we have established between us," he coughed to indicate this was hyperbole, "would certainly not survive such a betrayal. I would feel compelled to withdraw my offer of a reward under those circumstances and alternate methods of retrieval would be employed."

Wanda nodded. "That would certainly be unfortunate. But the thing of it is, Mr. Muscat, I just have your word that the ten thousand dollars even exists. You'll pardon my bluntness but you don't strike me as being a high roller. Someone who could draw on resources like that would have come with something a little more effective than an exhausted dragon tooth. For all I know this mysterious employer of yours might not even exist."

"I understand. Perhaps a token of my good will would be appropriate. Let's call it a retainer."

"You wish to establish a business relationship."

"Yes, certainly. I have one thousand dollars on my person."

"I know."

Muscat looked alarmed, then offended, then amused. "Of course. I should have realized. Would that be sufficient to retain your services on my behalf?"

"It's a start."

"Then if you do not personally have possession of the gargoyle, you might perhaps know where it is"

Wanda decided not to enlighten him just yet. "Can you prove that your employer is the rightful owner? I'm not hiring on to commit larceny."

Muscat bit his lip. "I'm not sure that I can do so to your satisfaction. As I explained earlier, it was brought into this country by unconventional means and there is no record of it here. I can only provide negative evidence. There is no one else in America who can establish any sort of legal claim."

"We'll let that pass for the moment, but I wonder if Mr. Thursday would argue the point if he was still capable of arguing about anything."

"Lloyd Thursday had no right to the gargoyle." Muscat sounded indignant.

"Is your employer here in Boston at the moment?'

"I have told you all that you need to know." He removed his wallet and counted out the thousand dollars, placing each bill carefully on the edge of the desk.

"Where can I reach you when I have something?"

"I will write down my address for you if you like."

Wanda took out one of her business cards and flicked it across the desk. Muscat smiled and took out his fountain pen, but instead of leaning forward to write anything, he pointed one end toward the middle of Wanda's chest. She was puzzled but only for a minute. There was no pain, no sense of alarm, no tactile impression whatsoever, but she could not move a muscle. "Don't be alarmed, Miss Coyne. It's a temporary spell with no unpleasant after effects."

Muscat scribbled something quickly on the card. When he was done, he stood up. "And now, Miss Coyne, I am going to search your office. He waved the pen at her. "Just in case."

She would have chuckled if she'd been capable of it.

Muscat had told the truth. She felt no transition at all. One moment she was frozen in place, the next she felt perfectly normal. Muscat was gone by then. He'd been frustrated by the office safe; otherwise the search had consumed only a few minutes. He hadn't spoken again before releasing the locking spell and slipping out of the office.

Her coffee was cold. She pushed it aside and picked up the phone. Poorhouse answered on the second ring. "Calling to confess your sins?"

"That would take some time. No, I wanted to ask about the Willett case? Who's handling it?"

"There's a team. It's high profile. Dandy's on it but I'm not. Masterton is in charge."

Wanda remembered that Masterton and Dandy hated each other. "I might have something for them. Do you think Dandy would talk to me?"

"Let's find out." Poorhouse put her on hold for a minute or so. There was a click and Dandy came on. "What's this all about, Coyne? I'm busy at the moment."

"Maybe I should talk to Masterton instead."

"Don't be cute."

She told him about the check written to Diana Marks. "Old news, Coyne. We got that from the people at the *Journal*. It wasn't on the body so we assume he mailed it before he was killed. Or delivered it in person. He was in the right neighborhood."

"Did she tell you what it was for?"

There was a pause. "We haven't interviewed the Marks woman yet. She hasn't been home. Why am I giving you information when you don't have anything to tell me?"

"Marks has been hanging around with the Whisperer."

"That's no secret, and no crime."

"No, but I also happened to notice that Taylor paid a visit to the widow yesterday. And someone called her while I was there last night and told her that her husband was dead and that was before the body was found."

"Are you sure of that?"

"Yes, but if she denies it, I have no way to prove otherwise."

"We'll talk to her. You might have to make a formal statement."

Wanda smiled to herself. "I'm at your service."

She heard Dandy clear his throat. "Thanks." It was grudging and almost inaudible.

"Just doing my duty as a citizen."

Her next call was to Alice Quinn. "What can you tell me about Diana Marks?"

"That was a rather unpleasant episode. It's not something I like to talk about."

"Make an exception. This is important. At least, I think it's important."

"You owe me for this one, Wanda. What do you want to know?"

"Everything."

"Will a summary do?"

"I suppose so."

"She was sexy, smart, ambitious, and hard working. That' the good part. She was also conniving, vindictive, ruthless, and sometimes cruel. I made allowances because she was good at her job and she seemed genuinely appreciative, but eventually it became obvious that it was all an act. She undermined my authority, talked behind my back, and she was setting up her own business even as I gave her more latitude here."

"Did you fire her or did she quit?"

"A little of both. She had a lot of talent. Some of my best customers used her exclusively. I lost some of them when we parted ways. The Begley twins. Omar Hadley. Myles Lewis."

"The deputy mayor?"

"He was only on the city council at the time."

"Well at least he never had a wife to cheat on."

"He was a regular and a big tipper. I hated to lose him."

"So she went out on her own."

"Yes, and she did quite well at first. But then she started losing girls. I think she decided she didn't need to keep up the act once she was the boss and there were some fights. When she broke Teri Bradon's jaw, it was the beginning of the end."

"Who's Teri Bradon?"

"She was one of mine originally, but she went with Diana when she left. Pretty girl, tiny like a doll, skin white as snow. I hated to see her leave but she had a crush on Diana."

"Was it mutual?"

"I don't think Diana actually likes, let alone loves, anyone but herself, but she did seem easier with our female clients than the males. I never did hear the details of her fight with Teri but there was an argument and Diana hit her across the face with a brass candlestick. Broke her jaw in two places. There was talk of prosecuting her for a while, but Bradon refused to press charges. She disappeared the day after she got out of the hospital. Rumor was she'd gone back to the Midwest, but another rumor was that she'd been reconsidering her decision not to talk to the police."

"Do you think Diana had her killed?"

"I wouldn't put it past her. In any case, she lost more girls and closed up shop a couple of months later. Freelanced on her own a bit with some of the better heeled clients. For the last couple of years she's been exclusively with the Whisperer."

"Any connection to the Willett family?"

Quinn sounded surprised. "I wouldn't blame Nathan Willett for cheating on that onion faced wife of his but I doubt it. And the old man likes boys."

"Really?"

"That's why he never remarried. His wife died young, you know."

Wanda asked a few more questions but learned nothing else of interest. Then Quinn had a question of her own. "Why the sudden interest?"

"Willett the younger paid her some money shortly before he died."

There was a whistle through the line. "Maybe I misjudged the man."

"I don't think it was for services rendered, or at least not those particular services."

"If it was blackmail, I'd have expected to find Diana dead rather than Willett. Unless it was self defense."

"He was shot in the back, several times."

"Point taken. You'll let me know when you find out what happened?"

"If I find out."

"You always find out, Wanda."

CHAPTER SEVEN

It was cold and windy so Wanda wrapped herself in a long coat for the walk home. She had her head down as she approached the entrance, but not so far down that she didn't spot the younger woman standing under a streetlight one building away. There wasn't anything overtly threatening, but it was chilly and uncomfortable, she was a block away from the bus stop, and two unoccupied cabs passed without being flagged down. Wanda stayed on the opposite side of the street and strode purposefully past with her face averted as though she had some place to be and that someplace wasn't here. There was a diner on the opposite corner and she had a cup of coffee and sat facing the street. The figure remained where it was for most of that time, then passed in front of Wanda's building and took up a position a few yards beyond.

"Very interesting," she said to no one in particular. She asked for a refill and ordered a sandwich.

By the time she'd finished, the mysterious figure had moved twice more but was still positioned to see anyone who entered the office building. On one occasion she had turned toward the diner and provided a good look at her face. Mildly pretty, slightly pinched features. Wanda had never seen her before. She was wearing an ornate broach on her jacket and every few minutes she tilted her head down to look at it.

Wanda asked for the check and took out the card where Muscat had written his address. It was the Blue Hippogriff, one step above being a dive. Muscat could probably afford better, but his profile would be smaller there. It was within walking distance. She considered hailing a cab anyway because the temperature was still falling, but decided that would make it unnecessarily difficult for the young woman to keep up. She walked past her building, paused to light a cigarette in full view of the watcher, then moved on toward the Blue Hippogriff without looking back.

The desk clerk didn't know, or wouldn't admit that he knew, Muscat's whereabouts but he grudgingly provided a room number in exchange for a five. There was no answer to Wanda's knock. When she came back down to the lobby, the mysterious young woman was sitting in a corner reading a two day old newspaper. Wanda smiled to herself and left.

This time she did hail a cab, which delivered her efficiently to the Arcanium. The show was already past intermission and the few people milling about in the gallery did not include Muscat. The café across the street was out of Wanda's usual price range but she mentally added it to the expense column and went inside for another coffee. It was good, but not that good. She drank it slowly while the young woman sipped an espresso a few tables away.

She spotted Muscat when he stepped out onto the street, hastily covered the check, and walked briskly over to intercept him before he flagged down a cab. Muscat blinked when he recognized her but was clearly not surprised. "My compliments on your thoroughness. You would have made note of the ticket. Is it too much to hope that you have already accomplished our mutual purpose?"

"I'm not sure how mutual it is, but no, I haven't. I want you to identify someone for me."

Wanda turned back toward the café, but the table where the young woman had been sitting was empty. She felt a few seconds of frustration before she spotted her quarry pretending to be window shopping at a charm and potion shop. "See the girl over there? The one with the dark red jacket and beret."

Muscat squinted and nodded.

"Who is she?"

"I haven't the faintest idea. Should I?"

"She's been following me ever since I left the office."

"It would seem to me, Miss Coyne, that someone in your profession might well have a number of persons interested in your activities for a variety of reasons. Have you considered that she might be from the police?"

"Too young, and too amateur."

"Associated with another client, perhaps."

"I don't think so." Other than Bridges, she had only one other client – assuming she could think of the late Nathan Willett as a client - and it was too soon for her to have made enemies in that matter. "You implied that other parties might be looking for the gargoyle."

"Yes, there are a number of collectors who would be very interested in acquiring it, and some of them are even less principled than myself."

Wanda let that slide. "Then you don't care if I take steps to rid myself of a nuisance?"

"If this person is an obstacle then I naturally applaud any effort you might take to remove her."

The crowd had largely disappeared by then and several cabs stood at the curb. Muscat nodded to Wanda and secured the first. Wanda waited until she was certain her tail was watching, then grabbed the second. The young woman was slipping into the third before they had turned the first corner.

When she reached home, Wanda slipped into warmer clothing, noting as she did so that someone had searched her apartment during the day. The police would not have tried to conceal their presence, so she ruled them out. It wasn't a professional job, but it was neat and orderly and she would have bet most of the thousand dollars in the office safe that it had been a woman. And she had a pretty good idea which woman.

She went outside without looking around and started walking along Jaeckel Street, almost able to feel the eyes on her back. Once again Wanda made no effort to throw off her shadow, even slowed her pace slightly when the crowds picked up. She paused in front of the Tiara and glanced around casually but was unable to spot the tail, although she was certain that she had not come alone, then continued along the sidewalk to the Nostradamus. There was some kind of convention going on, the Virginal Order of the Unicorn if she had to guess by the nametags, and she had to thread her way through the crowd to the rear. She recognized the security guard at the service entrance although she didn't know his name, nodded toward the door without speaking. He gave her a knowing look and opened it for her.

Wanda walked quickly down the alley and entered the Tiara from the rear.

Faye Bridges seemed happy to see her, but Wanda was well aware of her client's acting ability. She also noticed that Bridges seemed much more at ease in her expensive clothing this time and decided her earlier estimation had been short of the mark. The hotel room felt a little less formal this time. The suitcase was out of sight and clothing was visible in the small closet near the door. There was makeup and a hair dryer in the bathroom, a fashion magazine lay open on the bed, and a dreamcatcher hung in front of the window.

"Have you found out anything?"

"Possibly. I'm not sure that it's relevant to your situation."

"But you haven't told the police about me?" She took a step closer and Wanda could almost feel her breath.

"Not yet. Possibly not ever, but that remains to be seen."

"I'm at your mercy obviously. Why don't you sit down? I had some wine delivered." She walked over to the small refrigerator and took out a bottle. "I only have red, I'm afraid. I don't know much about wine but the hotel steward said this was a good one."

Wanda was pretty sure that was a lie, and an unnecessary one. Perhaps Bridges just enjoyed the parade of falsehood. She had been repeatedly forced to revise her impression of the woman. Anyone who dressed as expensively as Faye Bridges could probably identify fine wine by sniffing the cork.

"I only have these plastic glasses." She read the uncorking spell on the side of the bottle and it opened with a slight hiss.

Wanda sat down on the small couch under the window from which point she could watch the door and her client at the same time. There was a padded chair angled to one side but Bridges bypassed it, handed Wanda a plastic cup half filled with wine, then sat down beside her. Close beside her.

"You don't know how much safer I feel knowing that someone like you is looking out for me." There was a lilt in her voice that hadn't been there before and Wanda realized that it was meant to be seductive.

"You're full of surprises, aren't you?"

Bridges became coy. "Whatever do you mean?"

"I mean you wear personalities like some people wear clothes. If one outfit doesn't seem appropriate for the occasion, you switch to another, always looking to make the right impression."

Bridges leaned back and sniffed at her wine. "I never said I was on the side of the angels or that I can touch a unicorn."

"I wouldn't have believed you if you had. But I can't help if I don't have at least some idea of the truth."

"I understand." Maybe she did, but she still wasn't volunteering anything.

"Joe Muscat came to see me today."

Bridges was good at masking what she was really feeling, but not that good. Wanda saw surprise, wariness, and just a hint of fear before the mask settled back into place. "Is that name supposed to mean something to me?"

"You tell me. I just work here, or try to."

"I know of him." The words were coming very slowly. "Did he say anything about me?"

"We talked about a number of things."

"What did he want?"

"I'm guessing it's the same thing you want. He offered to pay me a great deal of money to acquire an object for him. A gargoyle."

"I see." Her voice shook and Wanda was pretty sure it wasn't an act this time. "And did you take the job?"

"Provisionally. You wouldn't have any objection if I did, would you? I mean, you haven't hired me to find it so there's no conflict that I can see."

Bridges set her glass down on the end table. Her hand was shaking but just barely. "You know there is."

Wanda took the time to taste the wine. She would have preferred brandy but it wasn't bad. "How would I know that? You've never said anything that would lead me to believe there's a connection between the two of you."

"You know there is or you wouldn't have brought it up. What do you want, Miss Coyne? A bigger retainer? A promise to match whatever Muscat has promised to pay you? I don't have the money with me but I can get it."

"I didn't expect you to have ten thousand in your purse."

"Ten thousand!" Bridges suddenly looked deflated. "I don't have that kind of money." She might have been talking to herself. "But I hired you first," she burst out. "Don't your professional ethics mean anything to you? Don't you have an obligation to me already?"

"Given the fact that the only time you haven't been lying to me is when you're refusing to answer my questions, as a result of which I've been charmed into immobility and shadowed for most of the day with no apparent reason for either, I think I should point out that ethics works both ways."

She looked abashed and Wanda wondered if it was genuine. "How can I convince you to help me? I can probably raise some more money. Not a lot."

"It's not the money. I'm just not sure that you even know what you're doing. I think you're making it up as you go along, and I know you're not telling me what I need to know if I'm going to help you."

Bridges hesitated. "I need to talk to Joe Muscat."

That surprised her a bit but she didn't let it show. "I can ask him to come here."

Bridges shook her head. "No, not here. I don't want him to know where I'm staying."

"There's my office."

"Too public."

Wanda fought down the urge to sigh dramatically. "What about my apartment?"

"I guess that would be all right. If you can get him to come there."

"He'll come." She glanced at her watch. "Why don't we head over there now and I'll call him when we arrive. That'll give you some time to decide just what it is that you want to say." Or to contrive another elaborate story.

"No. Not now. I'll come by your place in a couple of hours."

"Got a hot date?"

"I have to run an errand, yes. It has nothing to do with our business." That was almost certainly a lie but Wanda decided not to make an issue of it.

"You have the address."

"Yes, I do." Bridges seemed distracted and apparently was unaware of what she'd just let slip. Wanda didn't enlighten her but at least she had confirmed the identity of her burglar.

"See you then."

Wanday found a cab without difficulty. A block before they reached Wanda's building she saw the mysterious young woman walking in the same direction. A quick smile briefly disturbed her lips. Wanda paid the driver and went inside without glancing back to see if the woman was close enough to have seen them.

The phone was ringing. It was Captain Dandy. "Just thought I should balance the books and tell you what we found out based on what you told us."

Wanda was surprised at the courtesy, but only for a second.

"We got nothing. Mrs. Willett admits she got a call while you were there but says it was someone claiming to be from her husband's office telling her that he was working late. She was lying but we haven't got any leverage to use against her. Says she didn't know he was dead until she was officially notified. She doesn't like you, incidentally. She claims you were trying to bribe her husband into suppressing something juicy he found out about you and Bowman. I don't suppose that's true?"

"No."

"Well, we're going to have to poke around a bit anyway, so don't be surprised. Like I said, she was lying, but we might find something interesting anyway." He sounded almost cheerful at the prospect.

"Anything else?"

Dandy's voice changed and he spoke grudgingly. "Diana Marks finally turned up at her apartment. Said she'd been out of town on business all day and hadn't heard the news."

"You asked about the check?"

"Naturally. She says it was business, private business. A one time deal. That part might be true. This is the first time the *Journal* paid her anything and there's nothing in Willett's personal financials to suggest he was covering something himself."

"Do you think she was lying to you?"

"Everyone lies to us, Coyne."

Wanda hung up, glanced at her watch, picked the phone up again and called for a cab. Ten minutes later she was in the lobby of the Paracelsus, one of the most exclusive residence hotels in Boston. The desk clerk – who could have been a professional wrestler - was as daunting as Cerberus, refused a more than adequate bribe to call upstairs, but finally agreed when Wanda implied that she had been sent by the Whisperer.

"She says she never heard of you." The clerk had rung Marks' apartment.

"Tell her that I'm a friend of Nathan Willett."

The clerk spoke again, then hung up. "Room 1325."

"Do I need a charm or something to work the elevator?"

The clerk glanced up and Wanda followed his eyes. A wraithling hovered over her head, thin, insubstantial, ghostlike. Wraithlings were fashioned from the spirits of dead animals. They were not self aware but could be trained to perform simple tasks. "Do I give it a tip when it's done its job?"

"Just don't do anything that might piss it off."

"Why? Will it say 'Boo!' if I go someplace I shouldn't?"

"No, it'll just call for help. And the help in this place can be pretty ugly. Our head of security is a troll."

Diana Marks was tall and slender and quite beautiful. Wanda disliked her immediately, but not for those reasons. She was also supercilious and self absorbed. She opened the door and gestured for Wanda to come inside. The wraithling came as well, fluttered up to the ceiling and became almost invisible. "I hope you're not here to waste my time. It's the only currency that can never be repaid."

She hadn't been invited to sit, so Wanda brazenly dropped into the middle of an oversized couch covered with cashmere. "I hope I'm not wasting time for either of us, but that depends to a large extent upon how cooperative you are."

The apartment, what Wanda could see of it anyway, was lavishly furnished, a bit on the gaudy side and with no real sense of taste or pattern. There was an elaborate Victorian mirror with an intricately carved gilt border, a passably good landscape, a remarkably bad seascape, and drapes on the bay windows that clashed with the Persian carpet. The teak desk looked like an antique but the couch and matching chairs were very modern, all straight lines. The bar was constructed of stainless steel and polished brass. Marks crossed to the bar and poured herself a drink. Then, as an afterthought, poured a second and handed it to Wanda. It was scotch. Wanda hated scotch.

"You were a friend of Nathan's?"

"Actually, I never met him."

Marks' expression darkened. "Is this some sort of prank? Or are you a reporter?"

"No, and emphatically no. I did speak to him on the phone once. Like yours, my dealings with Nathan Willett were strictly business."

There was no softening of the other woman's features. "What kind of business?"

"I'm a private investigator."

"And what were you investigating for Mr. Willett?"

Wanda scratched her neck. "I can't really tell you that, Miss Marks. Client confidentiality, you know."

"But your client is dead."

"That does complicate matters, I admit."

"How does any of this involve me?"

Well, when I found out that my client was no longer in need of my services, I felt it only right that I express my condolences to his bereaved father. Said father would like to know who killed his son."

"So now you're working for Ezra?"

"Not exactly. It's all very complicated. But the thing of it is, I've been poking around and your name came up."

"I did see Nathan shortly before he was killed. We had some business to conduct. But it only took a few minutes and I didn't even know he was dead until the following day."

"He was just delivering the check then?"

Marks' eyes flashed angrily but her voice was cool. "That's right. I met him in the lobby, in fact. He never even came upstairs."

"The police think there's a connection."

"I can't help what they think. They're wrong."

"They also think maybe the Whisperer is involved."

"Why would they drag Max into this?" For the first time, she seemed less than sure of herself.

"He paid a visit to Mrs. Willett shortly after her husband's death."

"I don't know anything about that." Wanda couldn't tell if she was lying. Quinn was right; Diana Marks was talented. "If I had meant any harm to Nathan Willett, I would hardly have had him killed near where I live and minutes after I'd been seen with him."

"I didn't say that I believed you're involved. But the police do. And sometimes that colors the way they look at the rest of the evidence."

"So what's your interest?"

"Corny as it sounds, I'd like to know the truth."

Marks made a skeptical sound and rolled her eyes. "Noble, but noble doesn't pay the bills. I don't trust anything that doesn't have a price tag on it. And I don't waste time on something that doesn't benefit me."

"If I find out who really killed Willett, it would get the police off your back."

"How much is the old man paying you?"

"I can't talk about that, Miss Marks."

"And remind me why I should tell you anything."

"Because if you do and I find out who killed Willett, you're off the hook. Assuming that you didn't shoot him yourself. Otherwise, even if the cops don't pin it on you, they'll make your life miserable until they find someone else. And I don't think the Whisperer would much like the publicity either. He tends to be a very private person."

Marks sat back, considering. "I refused to tell the police what the check was for."

"Which only made them more convinced that it had something to do with the murder."

Marks chewed her lip. "I won't tell you anything specific but Willet wanted information that might cause some heads to roll, and sell a lot of newspapers. As it happens, I know a lot of things about some of our more prominent citizens that they would prefer not see in the morning headlines."

"Did he approach you or was it the other way around?"

"I might have suggested the possibility of an item of mutual interest to him earlier. We ran into each other every once in a while."

"Aren't you afraid that whoever killed Willett might come after you next? After all, cutting off the source is a more permanent solution."

"It wasn't like that. Sure, I could make life uncomfortable for some pretty powerful people. But they know better than to touch me. Max Taylor has ways of scaring people off. Most of the stuff was about small fry; the big fish would have wriggled a bit and stayed in the pool. All but one of them, and he deserved what was coming to him."

"Anyone I know?"

"Yes."

Wanda waited, but that was all she was going to get. "Did your boyfriend know what you were doing?"

"Max and I respect each other's space. I don't poke my nose into his business and he doesn't ask about mine."

"So when were you supposed to deliver the goods?"

"I handed him a flash drive when he showed me the check."

Wanda wondered briefly if the police had recovered it from the body. Dandy wouldn't have volunteered the information to her unless he thought it might help. But it didn't seem likely. They would have been more interested in Marks in that case. It was more probable that whoever had killed Willett had searched the body.

"I don't suppose you'd tell me who might have been inconvenienced if your information was in the news?"

Marks laughed. "Take your pick. The mayor, half the city council, Petra Finn, the chief of police, a couple of Congressmen, Alice Quinn, a few others. Everyone has something to hide."

"Even you?"

"Especially me, but I'm more careful than most of them."

Wanda glanced at her watch, then slowly stood up. The wraithling stirred above her head. "Thank you for your time. You've been a help, not a big help, but a help."

"I'm not used to giving away information for free."

"Maybe it's time you tried. You might start by warning Max Taylor that the police are looking into his business."

"He won't like that." She sounded unhappy, perhaps realizing that Taylor would also know that it was her shenanigans with Willett that had caused it.

"No one does."

CHAPTER EIGHT

Bridges was waiting outside the building when Wanda got back. "I buzzed your apartment but there was no answer. I was afraid something had happened to you."

"You're fifteen minutes early. You said eight."

"It didn't take as long as I expected."

They went inside and climbed the stairs. The phone was ringing when they arrived. Wanda pointed to a couch and picked up the receiver. It was Ava Bowman.

"I'm kind of busy at the moment, Ava. Let me call you back. Some time tomorrow."

"I've left messages at your office. Are you avoiding me?"

"I've just been very busy. We had a couple of cases working and now I have to handle them both by myself."

"I appreciate that, but this is important too. The insurance wasn't as much as I expected. I was hoping you could help me out. After all, you ended up with the agency."

Wanda sighed. "The agency is a rented office, some business cards, a filing cabinet and some used furniture, and a handful of unpaid bills, Ava. Should I send over half of the bills?"

"I know that things were tight. I wasn't looking to get something for nothing. I thought maybe you could take me on as, oh, I don't know, a consultant or something."

"And what would I consult you about?" Wanda had a feeling she knew where this was going, and Ava confirmed it quickly.

"Matthew used to talk to me about some of your cases, back when we were getting along better. He knew he could trust me to keep everything confidential. I want you to know that I know how to keep my mouth shut."

"That's good to hear."

"So any secrets you might have are safe with me. Particularly the kind of secret that might interest the police, if you know what I mean."

Wanda sighed again. "I have a pretty good idea." Ava still thought that Wanda had killed Bowman, or maybe she just hoped that was the case so she'd have some kind of leverage. "We'll talk again when I have some time. Good bye Ava." She hung up the phone.

It rang again almost immediately. "Miss Coyne? This is Sharon Llewellyn. You know, Mr. Willett's secretary."

"I know who you are. How can I help you?"

"I just wondered if you'd made any progress finding out what happened to Nathan. I guess it's just started to hit me that he's gone. He was a good man."

"Have you remembered anything else that might be useful?"

"Maybe. The police talked to me again today and they asked me if I'd ever heard of Max Taylor. I said no, because I hadn't, but then they told me he was the Whisperer and I knew that name of course. And then I remembered something strange that happened a few days ago."

"Strange in what way?"

"I put through a call to Mr. Willett one afternoon. It lasted about ten minutes, but I didn't actually hear any of it. Just after the line cleared, he came out and his face was white as a sheet. He told me to clear his calendar for the rest of the day and then he closed the door and I didn't see him again until the next morning. It wasn't like him. He was pretty brave in a quiet way."

"Did he ever refer to it again?"

"No. But you see, when I took the call originally, I had trouble understanding whoever was on the line because he talked in this really low, raspy kind of voice. Isn't that why they call him the Whisperer?"

Llewellyn had no more for her. Wanda thanked her and put the receiver down again. This time it remained silent.

Wanda called Muscat and got an immediate answer. "Coyne here. I have a Miss Bridges who would very much like to meet with you."

There was a long silence. "All right. You know where I'm staying."

"I'm afraid that won't do. Miss Bridges prefers a more neutral setting. My apartment is convenient to both of you."

"When?"

"She's here now if you're available. I assume you have my address."

"I know where you live."

Was it really Bridges who had searched her apartment, or was it Muscat? Or both of them, individually or together? "I thought you might. Shall we be expecting you then?"

"Half an hour." Muscat broke the connection.

Wanda had been watching Bridges out of the corner of her eye. She was obviously nervous. "Have you and Mr. Muscat known each other long?"

"Do you have anything here to drink?" It was an obvious ploy to avoid answering but Wanda decided to let it go for the moment.

"Brandy."

"Could I have some, please? I need to steady my nerves."

Wanda busied herself finding two matching glasses, then thoughtfully added a third, carrying them and a cut glass decanter of amber fluid back into the tiny living room. "I don't have any ice but I could cut it with water."

"No, that's all right." Wanda poured but Bridges was in no hurry to drink it now that she had changed the subject. They sat together in an increasingly uneasy silence.

Joe Muscat arrived right on time, but his face was twisted in unhappiness. "I assumed that this meeting was confidential, Miss Coyne."

Wanda shrugged and gestured him to come inside so that she could close the door. "There's a standard privacy spell protecting the building."

"Bah!" Muscat dismissed her statement peremptorily. "Easily penetrated by anyone sufficiently determined. That young woman you pointed out to me earlier is watching the front doors. She could be listening to us right now."

"That's entirely possible. Did she see you?"

"Of course she did. She's standing just outside the entrance."

"You said you didn't recognize her and there's no reason to believe she knows you. And given how inept her performance has been following me around, I doubt very much that she has any sophisticated magical gear hidden in her pockets."

Muscat didn't look convinced and Bridges had become agitated. "Who is this person you're talking about?"

Wanda shrugged her shoulders. "We haven't been introduced, but she's been following me around for the last day or so."

"Then she knows where I 'm staying!"

"Not unless she can read my mind. I made sure I'd lost her before I came by. I know that she's there, but I don't think she knows that I know. And frankly she seems more interested in me than in either of you, which demonstrates good taste but bad judgment. Take a seat, Muscat. You're making me nervous shifting back and forth like that."

Muscat took the single chair. Wanda decided not to sit beside Bridges – too adversarial – so she stayed on her feet. "There's brandy." She nodded to the decanter but Muscat shook his head, then turned to Bridges.

"Good evening, Faye. It's been a while."

"Yes it has."

There was a prolonged silence and Wanda poured herself a second brandy. Bridges seemed to be in the throes of some internal struggle, but one side apparently prevailed. "I understand you're offering ten thousand dollars for the gargoyle."

Muscat's expression sharpened and he nodded. "That is correct."

"In cash?"

"Of course. I would need a few hours warning, but the money is readily available. How soon would you be able to deliver the artifact?"

Bridges sat back. "Actually, I don't have it. Or at least not yet."

Muscat set his glass down. His hand was perceptibly shaking. "If you do not have it, why have we taken the risk of meeting?"

"I needed to have the terms of our arrangement spelled out. I'm taking as much of a risk as you are."

"You are wasting my time." But he made no move to stand up.

"You never were a patient man." Bridges was growing more confident now. "What would you say if I told you that I could have the gargoyle by this time next week?"

"Why the delay?"

"That's none of your concern. Will your offer still be good a week from now?"

"Of course. Unless I have acquired it through alternate means before then."

"That would be most unlikely. And perhaps unwise."

"Possibly, but why should I believe anything you say? I have only your word that you know where the gargoyle is."

"I know it all right. Lloyd told me." She sounded confident.

"Thursday had the gargoyle?" He almost hissed the words.

"That's what he told me. He said it was hidden in a safe place."

"And where would that be?"

Bridges laughed. "That would be telling, wouldn't it? Besides, he didn't exactly tell me where it is. But he hinted and I think I have it figured out."

"It makes no sense. Thursday knew what I was offering."

"Yes, but he figured he'd get a better deal if he bypassed you and went directly to your boss. Who is it, by the way? Matheson? Cowitt? Djanbe?"

"I am working for the rightful owner." Muscat managed to sound indignant and virtuous simultaneously.

Bridges raised her eyebrows. "Really? I didn't think he would take you back."

"The misunderstanding was cleared up." He hesitated. "As long as we're clearing the air, why are you willing to deal with me? You have at least as many contacts as Thursday. If I were in your place, I might consider playing the various parties off against one another in order to elevate the price."

"The thought had occurred to me, but it's too risky. I'd rather not have them poking around in my aura. And ten thousand is enough for me. I'm not greedy."

"Since when?"

"Since someone knocked off Lloyd. That wouldn't have been you, would it?"

Muscat shook his head. "Why would I kill the man who had it within his power to turn over the gargoyle?"

"You just said that you didn't know he had it. Or maybe you did after all, but Lloyd told you he was going around you to make his own deal."

"Nonsense."

"Perhaps. In any case, I'm planning to be a good deal more circumspect. I know better than to trust you. When I have the gargoyle, we'll make the exchange my way."

Muscat stiffened. "That may not be acceptable."

Her eyes flashed with anger. "It damn well better be or maybe I will decide to cut you out of the picture and deal direct. I still know how to reach him."

Muscat reached across with one arm like a striking cobra and grasped Bridges by the wrist. "Do not hope to play games with me. I'm not some flunky you can cast aside."

"Let go of my wrist or I'll claw your eyes out!"

Wanda decided this was a good time to intervene. She stepped between them, breaking Muscat's grip easily. For a second, it appeared that he was going to strike her, but he looked up into her face and thought better of it. "Perhaps it is time for me to go."

But before anyone could respond, someone knocked on the door. Bridges and Muscat both looked at Wanda, who shrugged. "Stay out of sight."

Lieutenant Poorhouse and Captain Dandy were standing in the hall. Dandy was fidgeting impatiently when Wanda opened the door, then stood squarely so that they couldn't come inside. "Isn't it past quitting time for you two?"

"We need to ask you a couple of questions," said Dandy. He shifted a foot as though to step over the threshold.

Wanda held her ground. "I was thinking of making an early night of it, but I can spare a couple of minutes. What do you want to know?"

"Let's go inside and sit." Poorhouse sounded uncomfortable. "We're just doing our job. Don't make it harder than it has to be."

"The place is a mess. I'd be embarrassed to have you see it."

"We've seen worse," said Dandy, shifting his weight again.

"I don't doubt it, but you're still not coming in."

"Did it ever occur to you that it might not be a good idea to piss us off, Coyne?" Dandy thrust his head forward so that she could feel his breath.

"Did it ever occur to you that people are more likely to cooperate if you don't threaten them for no reason."

Dandy ignored the riposte. "We've been talking to the widow Bowman. She doesn't appear to be any too happy with you. Seems she feels as though she was entitled for some compensation for her hubby's share of your business."

"Even if that was true, do you think it'd be worth her time to go after it, or mine to resist giving it up?"

Dandy must already have considered that angle because he nodded right away. "Point taken. But she hinted that there were other reasons why you might not be heartbroken by the turn of events. She thinks Bowman was over the hill, not carrying his share of the load even though he ended up with half the profit. Mrs. Bowman allows as how you might have good reason to resent the situation."

"Matthew pulled his weight. I had no problem with him. The Bowmans weren't on very good terms. She'll probably never forgive him for getting himself shot."

"Doesn't mean she's wrong."

"Anyway, I thought I was your top suspect for the Thursday killing. If I was the one who shot Matthew, that blows my revenge motive all to hell, doesn't it?"

"Maybe you killed Thursday so that we'd think he killed your partner."

"That's good. But then I'll have to kill someone else so that you think they killed Thursday, and then someone else to avert suspicion again. Not a very good plan."

"Yeah, well I never said you were a genius." Dandy made a mock casual move as though to slip past and Wanda put out on an arm, took hold of the door jamb blocking his way.

"You got something in there you don't want us to see?"

"Dirty laundry. Unwashed dishes. Overflowing wastebaskets. Dusty shelves."

"Funny. You missed your calling."

Poorhouse had been silent and increasingly uncomfortable. "Look, Wanda, we're not trying to pin this on you, but we have to do our jobs. Why are you making things so difficult?"

She felt sympathy for Poorhouse but didn't let it show. "I've cooperated as much as I can. I've answered your questions truthfully. If I knew anything that I thought might help you, I'd tell you." Eventually.

"But you won't let us in." Poorhouse sounded sad.

"No, not tonight. Maybe another time."

And then someone inside the apartment screamed and Wanda knew there was no point in holding them at bay any longer.

They found Muscat and Bridges glaring at one another. Bridges stood back against a wall, holding one arm awkwardly as though her wrist hurt. Muscat faced her but had retreated beyond easy reach; there was a line of blisters from the edge of his mouth to his right ear. On the floor between them lay what was unmistakably a firedrake shoot and, just beyond, an old fashioned stun wand.

"What's going on here?" Dandy stepped between them, while Poorhouse slipped around behind Muscat and retrieved the fallen items.

"They're trying to kill me," said Muscat defensively. "The two of them. They lured me up here and made me their prisoner. When that one went to answer the door, this one attacked me with the firedrake."

Bridges was not to be upstaged. "He's lying. As soon as I was alone with him, he pulled out a stun wand. If he hadn't waited to gloat first, he would have knocked me out and waited for Wanda to come back. It was just luck that I was suspicious and had the firedrake ready."

"I want the truth from the two of you and I want it fast." Dandy tried to roar at them but he didn't have the voice for it.

"I just told you," said Bridges.

"She's lying. It was the way I told it," said Muscat. "Tell them, Wanda. Tell them how it happened."

Wanda shrugged. "How would I know? I wasn't here, remember?"

"So why didn't you scream sooner, lady?" Dandy asked quietly.

"I didn't scream. He did." Bridges gestured toward Muscat, who looked abashed.

"We could take them all downtown and straighten it out there," suggested Poorhouse.

Wanda didn't like that idea at all. "I think I can clear things up here. Miss Bridges works for me."

Dandy and Poorhouse both looked skeptical; Muscat tried for outrage and did a fair job of it. "That's another lie!"

Wanda ignored him. "With Bowman gone, I needed some help with the legwork, at least temporarily. Muscat here tried to hire me to track down Lloyd Thursday's movements during the last week he was alive. Claimed Thursday was holding something for him and that he needed to get it back. Offered a sizable finders fee. But given that there's been the suggestion that I shot Mr. Thursday, I figured it might be a good idea to find out just what was going on before I decided whether or not to take him on as a client. So we asked him up here. I admit we grilled him pretty hard, but we didn't hurt him any. I guess he might have gotten some wild idea that we wouldn't let him leave, but he was mistaken."

Muscat looked sullen but he didn't respond.

Dandy, on the other hand, looked as though he might explode at any moment. "You're all coming downtown. We'll get to the bottom of this if it takes all night."

Wanda grimaced. "That's not such a good idea, Captain. You know the *Herald* has a clairvoyant monitoring the station around the clock. We'd make the news and it wouldn't be good for your career when everyone found out this was all just a practical joke that you were gullible enough to take a face value."

"Joke, huh? Well I'm not laughing, and neither are they."

There was a distinct pause, then Bridges began laughing softly, and reasonably convincingly. Muscat looked puzzled for another few seconds, then tried a chuckle that didn't work at all.

"You see how it is, Captain." Wanda walked over and poured herself a brandy. "The three of us were just having a drink together when the doorbell rang and we put together this little playact for your benefit."

"And I suppose this guy burned himself to make it look real."

"No, that was just an accident. I never said it was a good joke."

"I was explaining how it worked to Miss Bridges and it activated prematurely," added Muscat, warming to his role. "It was very stupid of me."

"You don't really expect us to believe any of this crap, do you?"

"What you choose to believe is your business, but you don't really think any of us is going to go on record by filing a formal charge."

Dandy spun on Muscat, correctly identifying him as the weakest link. "Well, you're coming with us in any case. Making a false statement to a police officer is a crime in this city."

Muscat extricated himself without assistance this time. "But I had no idea that you were a police officer. We planned and played out our little charade without ever seeing you, and for that matter, neither of you is wearing a uniform. We thought you were Wanda's friends."

Dandy turned to Bridges. "And I suppose you have a license to carry a firedrake?"

"As a matter of fact, I do. Would you care to see it?"

Dandy growled and spun to face Wanda. "You've gone too far this time, Coyne. I'm not the kind of enemy you want to have. I've been square with you up until now, but there are ways to deal with people like you."

Wanda felt her face flush and stepped toward Dandy. "Bring it on if you've got the guts for it. It'll take a bigger man than you to take me down."

Dandy was also red-faced, but Poorhouse stepped between them. "Cool down, both of you. This isn't the time or the place." He glanced at Bridges and Muscat. "We're leaving now."

For a second or two, Dandy seemed determined to continue the face off, but he relented. "Get their names and addresses."

Muscat offered his readily enough but Bridges just looked at Wanda. "Miss Bridges has just arrived in the city," she said at last. "We haven't found lodging for her yet. You can reach her through my office if you need to."

Dandy shook his head. "I want an actual address."

"Then we'll give you one as soon as she's settled."

They started toward the door and Muscat suddenly realized he was going to be left alone with Wanda and Bridges. "I think I'll be going as well. If I might have my wand back?"

Poorhouse started to hand it over, but Wanda intercepted. "You must have forgotten that I loaned you the wand, Joe. I'll just take it back now."

Muscat pouted but didn't contradict her. "Yes, I had forgotten. We will speak again, Miss Coyne."

"I'm sure we will."

Poorhouse handed the firedrake back to Bridges. "The charge is empty. You must have used this a few times already."

She made it disappear into her handbag without responding. Poorhouse nodded to Wanda and followed the other two men out the door.

Wanda took a full minute to recover her composure, then quietly poured herself a third brandy. Bridges had the good sense to keep her mouth shut and busied herself rearranging the contents of her bag. The brandy felt good going down, and Wanda turned slowly to face her remaining guest. "So just what went on in here while I was entertaining the city's finest?"

"He took out the stun wand, just like I said. I had the firedrake hidden under the cushion and I used it."

Wanda figured this was as close to the truth as she was going to get without some digging. "So what did you two talk about that set him off?"

"He wanted to make a deal and leave you out of it. I told him I wasn't interested."

"Will Muscat confirm that if I call him tomorrow?"

Bridges bit her lip. "I'm tired, Wanda, and I'm scared. Let me go back to my room and get some sleep. It's all mixed up in my mind and I need to straighten it out there first." She started to stand but Wanda moved suddenly, looming over her, and Bridges settled back onto the couch.

"I'll take the rough cut now. We can clean up the details later."

"I can't." Her voice was small, almost childish.

Wanda sighed. Obviously she wasn't going to get any further tonight. "All right, go. Say hello to my shadow on your way out."

Bridges blinked, seemed confused, then opened her eyes wide. "Do you think she's still down there? You said she was following you, not me."

"But she saw the two of us arrive together and she has to be following me hoping for a lead to someone else. That might be you, or she just might think it's you."

Agitated, Bridges looked around wildly as though someone might be lurking in a corner of the room. "Can't you help me?"

Wanda wanted to decline, but Bridges was, after all, her client. "Why don't I go down and check?"

Much to her surprise, the street was clear. If her shadow was still around, she'd suddenly acquired previously absent skills at concealment. Wanda actually hadn't cared either way; the trip downstairs was to clear her head and let her guest stew for awhile. It seemed to work because when she returned to the apartment, Bridges was standing in a shadow with the firedrake in her hand.

"She's still there," Wanda lied, closing the door behind her. "And now she has a friend. So they can watch both of us if they want." Bridges made an unhappy sound. "Maybe you should spend the night." She nodded toward the couch. "It's comfortable enough. And while you're here, you can tell me the whole story."

Bridges settled onto the couch again, but she was far from relaxed. "I'm not ready to do that."

"I'm going to find out sooner or later, you know."

"I believe you are, but I can't tell you everything. Not just yet."

"So what can you tell me?"

She shrugged. "Ask me a question. Maybe I'll answer."

Wanda thought for a moment. "Describe the gargoyle. What's it look like? How big is it?"

Bridges relaxed a bit. "It's about two feet tall, crouched, almost as though it was going to jump at you. Spiky ears, big eyes, knobby knees and elbows, claws on the feet and hands, bat wings half unfolded. You know, like a gargoyle."

"How heavy is it?"

"Not very. I could throw it across this room without much trouble."

"Color?"

"Dark, almost black but with coppery overtones."

"What's it made of?"

"Some kind of ceramic, with a metallic glaze."

"Why is it so valuable?"

Bridges shrugged. "I don't know, really. It's very old. No one ever told me that much and I didn't ask. But I do know it was stolen, although it didn't really belong to the other party either."

"Does this other party have a name?"

"Kemithor. He's a goblin."

Wanda blinked. Goblins rarely ventured out of Eastern Europe. "Where did all of this happen?"

But Bridges shook her head. "I'm not sure. Somewhere in Bukovina, I think. Lloyd might have known but he didn't tell me. We were just supposed to recover it and exchange it for our money, except that Lloyd claimed he was keeping it safe but I knew he had decided not to split the reward with me. That's why I wanted you to follow him. If I could get it away from him, he couldn't cheat me."

"But you could cheat him."

Bridges made no effort to look guilty. "It would have served him right, but I couldn't because I don't know how to contact the people who hired us." But she had earlier admitted that she knew how to contact its original owner.xxx

"And you're sure he really had it?"

"Oh yes, he showed it to me. That's why I know what it looks like."

Wanda digested that, then laughed. "That's quite a story. Holds together pretty well. How much of it is true?"

For a few seconds, Bridges looked offended, but she couldn't maintain the pose. "Some of it," she said at last. "I can't tell you everything yet. You know that."

"But you still expect me to help you."

Yes, I do."

Wanda stood and walked to the tiny closet, found a blanket and spare pillow, then tossed them to Bridges. "You can skip out during the night if you want, but I'm not going to tell you what our lady friend's partner looks like, so you'll be taking your chances."

Bridget looked down at the couch dubiously. There was a hole in one of the cushions and the dull gleam of a spring was visible. "I don't suppose you have a bed big enough for both of us."

"I'm not sure such a bed exists. You'll manage." Wanda put the brandy away, double checked the door locks, fed the door imp, and thought about going to bed.

CHAPTER NINE

The phone rang. It was Ezra Willett's secretary. "Mr. Willett would like to see you."

"Now? Does he know what time it is?"

"He keeps an unusual schedule. He was very insistent that he speak to you as soon as possible."

"So put him on the line."

"Mr. Willett does not care to use the telephone. He finds it too impersonal."

Wanda sighed. "Do you know how hard it's going to be to find a cab at this time of night?"

"That won't be necessary. I'm authorized to send a car to pick you up. Shall we say twenty minutes?"

"Yeah, okay." She was too tired to argue. Bridges was sitting up, looking inquisitive. "I have to go out for a while. Don't wait up."

The car was expensive but discreet, and so was the driver. He didn't try to start a conversation and Wanda actually dozed for part of the short drive to Back Bay. The secretary met her at the front door. Wanda yawned. "I hope he pays you well."

"Well enough. Wait in the library, please." There was an intensity about the woman that hadn't been there during Wanda's first visit. Something had changed.

It wasn't a long wait. The secretary returned almost immediately. "He's upstairs. Please follow me."

Ezra Willett was sitting in an oversized chair in a bedroom as large as Wanda's entire apartment. His face was composed but there were lines of tension that hadn't been there earlier.

"You wanted to speak to me?"

He nodded. "But first I want you to see something. Over there, on the balcony."

The secretary pointed and Wanda moved toward the opening where a full set of thick drapes moved restlessly in the breeze. The balcony had a waist high railing, a couple of potted plants, two lounge chairs and a round table, all wrought iron, and a dead body. The face was turned to one side; Wanda didn't recognize it. A pool of blood spread like an inky shadow among the inky shadows.

"I wouldn't want one of these on my balcony, if I had a balcony. Who is he?"

The secretary looked insulted. Ezra gave a short laugh. "I don't know who he is but I know what he is and what would have happened if I hadn't been awake."

"How did he get past security?"

"He didn't. His levitation spell triggered three separate wards. I shot him as he came over the railing."

"Did you piss someone off recently?"

"No more than usual."

Wanda patted him down. There was a handgun in a shoulder holster, a kris knife taped to one wrist, and a functioning dragon's tooth in a pocket, along with a variety of amulets and tokens, most of which she couldn't identify.

"He was well equipped."

"But not very competent. This might have been meant as a warning rather than a serious effort to kill me."

"A warning from who? And about what?"

Ezra shrugged. "I have a lot of enemies, but we've worked out an arrangement of sorts. I suspect this might be connected to the death of my son. We weren't on the best of terms, but that wouldn't stop me from asking pointed questions about his death."

"So why am I here?"

"We talked about the possibility of my retaining your services."

"No, you talked about it. As I recall, I turned you down."

"I usually get what I want."

"Glad to hear it. But life has its little disappointments."

"Name your price. Everyone has a price."

"I agree, but sometimes that price isn't measured in dollars." She sighed. "But I want to know who killed your son. He wasn't even a client yet, technically, but he was going to be."

"Then you'll take the job?"

"Against my better judgment and with reservations. But whatever I find out goes to the police unless I decide otherwise."

"What would you consider to be an adequate retainer?"

"Let's say a thousand even."

Ezra turned to the secretary. "Make it two thousand." Wanda opened her mouth to object, but he waved her off. "When the job is done, you can give back whatever portion of it you feel you haven't earned."

Wanda glanced back at the body. "What about this gentleman?"

"Anita here will call the police and tell them we've just had an unfortunate encounter with a burglar. I imagine you would prefer to be gone before they arrive."

"That would be simpler, yes."

"The driver will take you back. Good night, Miss Coyne."

When Wanda got up early the following morning, Bridges was curled up at one end of the couch, so soundly asleep that she didn't stir while Wanda made and drank a cup of coffee. Nor did she give any sign of awareness when Wanda looked through the contents of her handbag, which included the firedrake, a couple of charms she couldn't identify, and the usual things a woman would carry around with her. There was also a hotel key, which Wanda pocketed. Thoughtfully, she left the coffee things out for her guest, then left the apartment.

There was no sign of her shadow as she walked to the Tiara. She nodded to the desk clerk, who barely glanced up, then went directly to Bridges' room and unlocked the door. She moved quickly but systematically, opening drawers and sorting through their contents. She unmade the bed and looked under the mattress, examined the grill and shower head for signs of tampering, looked under and behind the furniture for items taped in places where they couldn't be seen. She made no effort to conceal the fact that the room had been searched and she found nothing of interest. When she was finished, she opened the window leading to the fire escape, closed it behind her, then wrapped her fist in her coat and broke one of the panes. The glass fell down inside the room. Satisfied, she climbed down and started home, stopping on the way for a box of doughnuts.

Bridges was awake and drinking coffee when Wanda opened the door. She looked vaguely suspicious until Wanda showed her the doughnuts. Her face relaxed but her body didn't. "I checked around the neighborhood. Our two new friends both seem to have gone away for the moment."

"Are you sure?"

"I'm a trained professional, remember? And I was pretty thorough. I went over the whole block twice and poked my head into every place that was open for business."

"Maybe they weren't following you after all."

"Maybe. There are clean towels if you want to shower."

Bridges shook her head. "Thanks, but I'll just fix my face before I go." She closed the bathroom door and Wanda quietly dropped the hotel key into her handbag.

"I don't suppose you feel more like telling me the truth this morning?"

"Not particularly," came the voice through the door. "Be nice and don't push it, all right? I'm not feeling great. Your couch has some loose springs."

"Your call."

Wanda went downstairs with Bridges and glanced around. There was no sign of the young woman. She hailed a cab and put Bridges into it. "I'll call you later." Bridges nodded and the cab moved away. Wanda waited until it was out of sight before hailing another. "Take me to the Blue Hippogriff."

The young woman was there, eating breakfast in the lobby café, seated so that she could watch everyone coming in or going out. If she noticed Wanda, she gave no sign of it. The desk clerk ignored her as well until she cleared her throat, then grudgingly told her that Joe Muscat was not in his room. "No, I have no idea where he is. It's not a house rule that the guests tell us their private business."

Wanda hated wasting a trip so she talked to a man she knew who worked at the hotel, then stepped into the café. The hostess started toward her, but Wanda waved her off. "I'm meeting a friend." Then she walked over to the young woman's table and sat down without waiting to be invited.

"I thought it was time we met officially."

The young woman gave her a belligerent look. "I beg your pardon. I've never seen you before."

"Awww, come on. That's no way to act. I feel like I've really gotten to know you over the last couple of days."

"I have no idea what you're talking about. Please leave my table."

Wanda made a sound of regret. "I don't suppose you want to tell me about it? That would make things much easier."

"Look, I don't know who you are but if you don't leave me alone, I'm going to have the waitress call security and have you thrown out."

Wanda smiled. "That's an excellent idea, but we don't have to involve the waitress. We can go direct." She waved to the man she'd talked to a moment before, who was somewhat awkwardly standing near the cash register. His sour expression deepened as he approached.

"I was right, Luke. This is the woman I saw picking pockets at the Nostradamus last month. She's probably waiting for the lobby to fill up."

The young woman looked alternately furious and nervous. "I have no idea what you're talking about. I've never seen this woman before and I've never even been to the Nostradamus."

"Are you a guest of the hotel, Miss?" asked Luke.

"No, not at the moment. But the café isn't reserved for guests. I have a perfect right to be here."

"Could I see some identification please?"

The chair clattered backward as the woman stood up abruptly. "I don't have to put up with this. You have no right to question me." She started to brush past Wanda, who put out an arresting arm.

"Didn't you forget something?"

"What?"

Wanda gestured at the half eaten breakfast platter. "You need to pay for your meal."

For a second it looked like the confrontation would become physical, but the woman finally jerked open her handbag, took out a few bills, and tossed them on the table. "Don't forget the tip," said Wanda, but the woman was already walking away, back rigid.

"Thanks for the heads up," said Luke.

"No problem. Hey, I got a question for you. Do you know anything about one of your guests? Joseph Muscat." She provided his room number.

"Come with me."

Wanda followed him to a dingy office. She was expecting another crystal ball, but the Blue Hippogriff was more sophisticated.

There was a computer terminal. Luke punched a few keys, frowned. "Nothing special. He's been here five days." A few more clicks. "The maid says his bed wasn't slept in last night, but he hasn't checked out."

"Interesting."

"Yeah, but it happens. I'll keep an eye on him if you want."

"If you can, but don't make a career out of it. He's a client, sort of. I was just curious. I guess I'll have to wait for him." She looked around and moved to an empty table.

Luke intercepted the waitress. "Her meal is complimentary."

Wanda had finished eggs and toast and bacon and was on her second cup of coffee when she saw Muscat walk into the lobby. She left a generous tip and moved to intercept him. The burns on his face were almost invisible so he'd obviously visited a healer.

"Morning, Joe."

Muscat sniffed and turned away from her.

"We need to talk."

"I don't think either of us has enjoyed our previous attempts at conversation. Why should this one be any different?"

"Are you still sore about last night? You know that wasn't my fault. The cops were ready to throw us all into the lockup. And I have to play up to Bridges if she's ever going to tell me where the gargoyle is."

"You think she has it?"

"Someone does. It might as well be her." Wanda paused. "Dandy took you down to the station after you left, didn't he?"

"He was most insistent."

"They give you a hard time?"

"It was not pleasant. I was released only a short time ago and would very much like to shower and sleep."

"How much did you tell them?"

Muscat looked genuinely affronted. "Do you take me for a fool? I kept to your story, of course, ridiculous as it was. Couldn't you have thought of something more plausible?"

"I was a bit pressed for time."

Eventually Wanda made it to the office, where Perry gave her a hurt look. "Ava called. Twice." He jerked his head toward her office door. "Miss Crest or Bridges or whoever she is arrived a few minutes ago. I told her she could wait."

"Anything else?"

"Lieutenant Poorhouse called and asked if you'd ring him back. He didn't say why. And another man called. Wouldn't leave a name, but said you should be kinder to a poor young girl who is just trying to make an honest living."

"Did he leave a number?""

"No. He said he'd be in touch later."

Bridges stood up the moment Wanda opened the door. Her face was pale and her eyes wide. "Someone searched my room last night!"

Wanda kept her face immobile. "Did they take anything?"

"No, I don't think so. It must have been that woman, or her partner. They must have followed you there when you came by earlier."

"I am sure of very few things in this world, Miss Bridges, but I am certain that I was not followed to your hotel."

"Then who could it have been?"

"You're probably in a better position to answer that question than I am. Maybe the gargoyle's presumed owner had more irons in the fire than you thought. Or maybe it was Joe Muscat. I stopped by his hotel today and they said his bed hadn't been slept in."

"Why were you at his hotel?"

"I wanted to make sure that my friend Captain Dandy hadn't gotten him to break down and tell the truth about our little charade last night. He came in just as I was leaving and claimed he'd been with the police all night but that he hadn't talked. I'm not sure I believe him, but then I'm not sure I can believe anything I've been told about this case."

Bridges turned away. "I'm afraid to go back to the hotel. I'll have to find another place to stay."

Wanda nodded. "Wait here." She went back to the outer office. "Perry, do you have a spare bedroom?"

"Sure. We hope to make it a nursery one of these days."

"Would your wife mind a paying guest for a while?"

"Well, you pay me such a princely salary that we really don't need the money, but yeah, I think she could be talked into it." He glanced toward her office. "Our lady of many names?"

"Yes. She's been burglarized twice since she first came to see us so she needs a place where no one is likely to find her."

"Is she in any danger?"

"Probably."

"Well, I won't tell Julia that part."

CHAPTER TEN

Perry went off with Bridges to retrieve her luggage, leaving Wanda alone in the office. So she was the one who picked up when Lieutenant Poorhouse called. "You scored a few points with Masterton, Wanda. He sort of hinted that Dandy and I shouldn't give you a hard time unless it was necessary."

"Nice to know the man has a sense of gratitude. Are you looking at the Whisperer for the Willett murder?"

"You know that if I was working that case, I'd be forbidden by department policy from divulging any of the details of an ongoing investigation."

"Yes I do. But you're not on the task force, are you?"

"Nope."

"So the rules don't really apply."

"That's one possible interpretation."

"I gave something to the department. Don't I get a quid pro quo?"

"It's too big to sit on anyway. Dandy and Masterton led a team over to the Belltower."

"That's Taylor's mansion, isn't it?"

"Residence and place of business. It used to be a funeral home and crematorium."

"I'll bet he bakes his own bread."

"Anyway, there was a troll standing guard at the gates and he refused to open them because Masterton didn't bother to ask for a warrant. Dandy's got a short fuse though and he started threatening to force the gate and you know what happens when you threaten a troll."

"They get angry. And stubborn."

"This one got so mad he refused to even call the house. Masterton said Dandy and the troll traded insults through the gate for ten minutes before he could get Dandy to back off."

"And the upshot of all this was what?"

"Masterton finally decided to go for a warrant, but before he could leave the Whisperer himself showed up. He kept the gate closed but he was willing to answer a few questions. Masterton was almost as pissed as Dandy by this point but the two of them calmed down eventually. Then they talked through the fence for a while."

"Did they kiss and make up?"

"Not really. Taylor admitted that he visited Mrs. Willett to express his condolences but wouldn't explain his connection to her, just said that they are acquainted. He was even less forthcoming about Diana Marks and characterized her as a friend. Masterton stayed cool but Dandy frustrates easily and he came close to accusing the Whisperer of killing Willett because the dead man was fooling around with his girlfriend. Taylor found that pretty funny and then asked Masterton for the precise time of death. It turned out that he was at a meeting of the Sorcerers' Council at the time. That doesn't mean he didn't hire someone to do the job, but it does mean that Masterton has no grounds for a search and has to eat pie abd that got him mad as hell."

"Anything else?"

"Not yet. You getting anywhere about Bowman's killer? Off the record, I know it wasn't you."

"Thanks. I'm not sure. I'll be in touch."

Wanda hung up, then wrote a brief note for Perry asking him to check into the background of Mrs. Gladys Willett.

A year old issue of *Thyme* magazine was on her desk with a note from Perry. "Look at page 33." The reference was to a profile of Nathan Willett, who had doubled the *Journal*'s circulation in less than two years. There was a picture of him attempting to smile, standing in his secretary's office. Sharon Llewellyn was there but she seemed even more uncomfortable than her boss, had turned her head away so that only her profile showed. Wanda tore out the page, folded it carefully, and put it in her pocket.

Moments later the phone rang. She didn't recognize the deep voice of the man who identified himself as Mr. Goodman. "Is that really your name?"

"Does it matter?"

Mr. Goodman would very much like to meet with her but no, her office would not do, could she possibly visit him at his room? He was currently staying at the Imperial. "When?"

"As soon as possible."

She had barely replaced the receiver when the door opened and Ava Bowman came in. "Wanda, I'm so sorry. I just wasn't

thinking when I talked to Captain Dandy and I may have said
something that led him to think you might be responsible for
Matthew's death. I hope I haven't made things difficult for you."

"No more than usual."

Ava considered that, decided to ignore the implication.
"Grief does things to people, you know. I never expected to grieve
for Matthew, but now that he's gone, I realize how much I've lost."

"Knock it off, Ava. You might be able to fool Dandy with the
act, but I know better. You found a replacement for Matthew a long
time ago."

Ava looked shocked. "What are you saying? Are you
accusing me of something?" Her thoughts suddenly flew off in
another direction. "What do you know about me anyway?"

Wanda was too disgusted to try to soothe things over.
"Where were you the night Matthew was killed, Ava? I know you
weren't at home."

Ava looked shocked. "You don't think that I had anything to
do with Matthew's death, do you? That's absurd!"

"So where were you? Spending an evening with your lover?"

The look of offense was transparently phony. "So maybe I
took a walk that night, went looking for some company. I might have
had a couple of drinks, chatted up some guys, but nothing came of it.
I wasn't unfaithful, despite what you might think."

"I don't think anything, Ava. I just wonder."

"Well now you know."

"Okay, you've convinced me. But you might want to work on
some of the details of that story because Captain Dandy might be a
lot harder to convince."

"You can't think he suspects me of doing anything wrong?"

"Dandy suspects everyone of doing something wrong. Go
home, Ava." And after a brief hesitation, that's what Ava did.

The room number Goodman had provided was a suite at the
end of a long corridor. Wanda knocked on the door and was not
surprised when it was opened by the young woman she'd humiliated
that morning. Smiling, Wanda pushed past and found herself in a
sumptuous room with a recessed seating area. Sitting in a straight
backed chair was the tallest, thinnest man she had ever seen. He was
easily seven feet but she doubted that he outweighed her. He had

bushy black eyebrows that seemed too big for his face and a sardonic and patently insincere smile.

"Come in, Miss Coyne. Or do you prefer Ms? My name, at least for our present purposes, is Goodman. I apologize for not rising but I have a troublesome hip problem which makes standing up and sitting down both quite painful."

Wanda stepped forward and descended the three steps. "It's nice to meet you, Mr. Goodman," she lied. "And I prefer just Coyne if you don't mind."

"So be it. Names are such inconsequential things. It is only our true names that count, and they are so rarely revealed. May I offer you a drink? I believe you prefer brandy." The young woman had already crossed to a small bar and was pouring amber liquid into a glass. She wasn't smiling when she handed it to Wanda.

"Please sit down. There is, I think, much for us to talk about so make yourself as comfortable as possible."

"What would you like to talk about, Mr. Goodman? This is your party."

"I think you might have some idea of the subject matter in which I'm presently interested."

"Would it have an ugly face and an empty head?"

Goodman lowered his formidable brows. "That's an odd way of describing it, but yes, I'm interested in its present location."

Wanda's eyes moved to the young woman. "She's standing right there."

The woman clenched her jaws. Goodman looked puzzled, then amused. "Clever, but you've made your point." He waved and the woman gave Wanda a look that promised retribution, then retreated out of sight. "I assume you are authorized to speak for Miss Bridges."

"In a manner of speaking. I'm in a bit of a quandary here, Mr. Goodman. Through no fault of my own, I seem to have taken on two clients with conflicting desires, so you can understand my reluctance to commit myself."

"You refer to Mr. Muscat?"

"I can't reveal the identity of my clients."

"If you wish to maintain that façade, feel free to do so, but we all know that they are the only parties concerned with this matter."

"You're wrong about that."

Goodman's expression said that he very much doubted that he could be wrong about anything. "Who else is there?"

"My partner was murdered and I'm suspect number one. I think that makes me an interested party."

"Regrettable, but Mr. Bowman's death and your subsequent difficulties may be entirely unrelated, and they are certainly of no interest to me, if you don't mind my saying so."

"I don't mind at all, but I don't grant your premise either."

"There we shall have to agree to disagree."

"So where does that leave us?"

"Where we started. The gargoyle. Do you have any idea of its potential importance?" His voice deepened and he leaned toward her.

"Only a glimmering. I gather that it's a valuable artifact of dubious provenance."

Goodman blinked, then laughed. "I do believe that you are totally ignorant of the gargoyle's true nature. Is that not so?"

Wanda paused, but she could only push her bluff so far. "I'm not completely in the picture, but I understand that it's important enough to have cost at least two lives already."

"So Miss Bridges has not been completely open with you?"

"I doubt openness is numbered among her talents."

Goodman laughed again. "She is in some ways a very delightful lady but, as you say, not very forthcoming even when it's in her own interests. I hope this is not a quality you share. And I gather Mr. Muscat was similarly secretive?"

"Mr. Muscat doesn't like me very much and tells me as little as possible."

Goodman was lost in thought for a few seconds. "It is very unlikely that they don't know at least part of the truth, but I suppose they may not be as well informed as I assumed. More likely they are simply unwilling to reveal how much they know." He was silent for another few seconds. "If, on the other hand, they are truly ignorant of the gargoyle's nature, it makes my position in this affair considerably stronger."

"I'm glad for you."

"Charming though you may be, I confess that I see no purpose to this meeting if you are as badly informed as you appear to be. No offense intended, but I believe in speaking candidly. I don't see that you have anything to offer me."

"I have one thing."

"And what would that be?"

"I know where the gargoyle is."

"Ah, I see. And what is your price for divulging this information?"

Wanda sipped her drink. It was good, better quality than she could afford. "Now you see, that's where we have a problem. As you correctly pointed out, I am woefully ignorant of the value of the item in question, so I find myself incapable of naming a price. On the other hand, if someone were to explain its importance, I would be in a better position to assign a cost to my services in recovering it."

"So what you propose is that I tell you what I know gratis, as a consequence of which you will be better prepared to negotiate terms. That hardly seems fair."

Wanda shrugged. "Fairness isn't necessary in a business arrangement. Besides, the proposition isn't as one sided as you imply. You have the contacts and knowledge to realize the gargoyle's potential. I don't. You're going to make a lot of money on this deal. Can you blame me for wanting a small piece of the pie for myself?" She set the glass down and stood up. "Why don't you think about it, Mr. Goodman, and get back to me?"

As if summoned by magic, as might have been the case, the young woman reappeared, her expression grim. She had one hand in her pocket. Wanda hardly glanced at her. "And keep this flunky of yours away from me. She's lousy at her job and she's so obvious that she scares my clients." She walked to the door, put a hand on the knob, then glanced back. "But don't think too long. I might know a couple of other people who'd be interested."

Goodman frowned. "You're bluffing. No one else could possibly know that it is not still in Europe."

"You might be surprised." Wanda left, wondering if she'd overplayed her hand.

CHAPTER ELEVEN

Very conveniently there was a cab waiting in front of the hotel. Wanda got inside and immediately realized that it wasn't happenstance. The windows were pitch black and the sounds of the city were cut off as if with a switch. The driver had the perfect skin and unblinking eyes of a homunculus and while the back seat had appeared empty from outside, she found herself sitting next to a tall man swathed in black.

"Mr. Taylor, I presume?"

"In a manner of speaking, Miss Coyne." His voice sounded muffled and was barely audible. He raised a hand and extended it toward her. It passed through her arm with no sense of contact.

"Astral projection? Isn't that a bit showy?"

"It is also somewhat uncomfortable, but it saves me the time I would have wasted sitting here waiting for you to appear."

"You've had me followed."

"Located, not followed. It's not one of my more proficient talents, unfortunately. I understand you have been speaking to the police about me."

"I told them that I had seen you visit Mrs. Willett."

"They believe that I had something to do with his death."

"They're anxious to close the case for political reasons. I'm not sure that they care if they actually get the right person. You know that Willett was connected to Diana Marks."

"The police mentioned the matter. I don't presume to know all of Miss Marks' business. We are just friends, not intimates."

Wanda raised an eyebrow, but was ignored. Maybe he was telling the truth. "So what do you want from me?"

"I understand that you are investigating Willett's death."

"That's right. If you didn't do it, why are you interested?"

"I would not like to see Mrs. Willett troubled any more than she already has been. I would take it amiss if you were to harass her, or take any action that might lead to that result."

"Do you think she killed her husband?" That couldn't be right; Wanda was the widow's alibi. "Or had it done for her?"

"Mrs. Willett loved her husband, in her own way. But some aspects of their relationship were unconventional. Suspicious minds might interpret this incorrectly."

"Then she has nothing to worry about from me. Unlike the police, I'm not interested in just closing the case."

"Then what are you interested in?"

"I don't know. Justice, maybe. Whatever that is."

"The concept of justice exists in my field of expertise, but it has no reference to written laws. It is more a sense of balance."

"Yeah, I like that. I'm looking for balance. Willett's death tilts the scales. I want to level them out."

The door suddenly swung open. "I believe we understand one another."

Wanda didn't move. "I don't suppose you could drop me off at my office?"

The Whisperer turned to look at her directly for the first time. His face was heavily lined and his complexion was darker than she'd realized. "Of course, but you'll have to excuse me if I don't accompany you. I have rather a busy day ahead of me." And he vanished without a sound.

The door closed and the cab moved out into traffic.

Sam Bowman, Matthew's brother, was waiting for her at the office. Sam was the younger brother and looked almost nothing like his sibling. He was tall, dark, and handsome, or had been a decade earlier when he and Wanda had burnt their way through a three month romance. Fortunately, they had both lost interest at the same time – not surprising since Sam was a sensitive - and parted on good terms. Wanda gave him a hug, lied and told him he was looking great.

"Other than the receding hairline, expanding waistline, and emerging wrinkles, I suppose you're right. But you really do look great, Wanda. The years have been kind."

"Not really, but it doesn't all show. I'm sorry about Matt. I feel kind of responsible. It was my client he was working for."

"Matt was destined to die on the job. I imagine he's pleased with himself, wherever he is now."

"I hope so. You've seen the grieving widow."

"Well, I've seen Ava." Sam had never liked Ava, even when she and Matthew were getting along. "That's why I came to see you. Or at least it's one of the reasons I came to see you."

"She thinks I did it, you know."

"No, she doesn't. She wants it to be true because it would give her some leverage, but she knows it's nonsense. She was jealous of the two of you."

"Matt and I? We never even flirted."

"Not that kind of jealousy. The two of you were close. I don't think she's ever experienced that with another human being."

"Her loss. So how long are you going to be in Boston?"

"The cremation is tomorrow and I'm leaving right afterwards. But I wanted to see you. I had a long talk with Ava and she told me some things that you need to know. Except she doesn't know she told me."

"Something about Matt?"

"About the night he was killed. You know my sensitivity is pretty low, but her emotions are like sirens going off. She'd say one thing and radiate an entirely different meaning. I'm afraid I plied her with liquor to lower her inhibitions, but it was obvious that she was hiding something important, something that terrified her, and I thought I should find out, for her own safety. As it turns out, it wasn't her safety I needed to worry about."

"You're not telling me she knows who killed Matt?"

"No, nothing like that. But she was following him the night he was killed."

The idea of Ava Bowman shadowing anyone felt unlikely but Wanda had to admit there was a slyness to the woman that surpassed her intelligence. "Why would she do that?"

"She thought he was having an affair and she wanted proof."

"Why? She could have divorced him a long time ago. He wouldn't have fought it and he'd have let her take everything they had, which wasn't much." The idea of Bowman conducting a clandestine sexual liaison struck her as funny. "So how much did she see?"

"She followed him to some hotel, but I couldn't get the name. She was afraid to go in so she went to a bar across the street and had a few drinks. Quite a few drinks, apparently, because everything's a blur after that. The only other thing I could read is that she went to your place."

"My place?"

Sam nodded. "The door guardian wouldn't let her in so she went home. Or I think that's what happened. Most of her memories are confused until Perry and his wife showed up to tell her that Matt was dead."

"Could she have followed Matt again when he came out of the hotel?"

"It's possible, but I don't think so. If you're thinking that maybe she killed him, I'd say it was pretty unlikely. That would have left a mark on her psyche that even I could have read. She' has one of the weakest auras I've ever encountered."

"Anything else?"

"No, sorry. I'm heading home tonight and I wanted to make sure you knew before I left." He got to this feet and she stood as well.

"All right. Thanks for coming by."

"My pleasure. If you're ever down in Providence…"

"I have your number."

Five minutes after he left, Perry came in. He looked unhappy. In fact, he looked furious.

"She ditched me!"

Wanda felt a surge of frustration and anger. "Bridges? What happened?"

"I got us a cab and we stopped to pick up her stuff. Then on the way out to Brookline she asked if we could stop and get some bottled water. I hopped out and bought some and when I got back to the street, the cab was gone."

Wanda thought about it. It didn't seem to make sense, but it was certainly in character. "All right, she's gone to earth somewhere on her own again. I'll just have to find out where. I don't suppose you remember the cab number?"

Perry smiled and took a slip of paper out of his pocket. "As a matter of fact, I did."

It took a while, and fifty bucks, to convince the cab company to cooperate but Wanda finally connected with the right driver. She described Bridges and the stop for the bottled water.

"Yeah, I thought there was something fishy about that." The driver was a redhead with tattoos down both arms. "She said she'd changed her mind. I asked if we should wait for the other guy but she said it was no problem. And she paid me to forget about him."

"Where did you take her?"

"She paid me to forget that too."

"How much would it take to refresh your memory?"

She asked for a hundred, settled for half. "She got out at the Faerie Building."

"Did she go inside?"

"Yeah, but I got a fare right away so I don't know if she went upstairs or just stayed on the shopping level."

"What about her luggage?"

"She only had one bag and it wasn't that heavy."

There were at least a dozen exits from the Faerie Building. Wanda considered the possibilities, decided it would be a waste of time to try to track her own directly, and started back to the office instead. But she never made it there.

Goodman's young friend was waiting for him in the lobby, her hands deep in the pockets of her overcoat. "Mr. Goodman would like to talk to you."

"What if I have nothing to say to him?"

One hand came out of a pocket just long enough so that Wanda could see what it held. "A Saturday Night special? Goodman must get his flunkies from the Salvation Army."

"Very funny. It might not make a hole as big as a salamander would, but it'll get the job done."

"And it doesn't require any brain power to use it, which is a plus for you."

"You know, sooner or later this business will all be over with, and then maybe you and I will have time to deal with personal issues."

"If Goodman lets you off your leash, you mean."

"You talk a lot, Coyne. So let's go talk to Mr. Goodman."

Wanda led the way across the short hall to the doorway. She had just reached for the outer door when she heard a low cry from behind her. The other woman was bent forward, clutching her belly with both hands, one of which still held the revolver. Her shoulders were shaking and she made retching sounds. Wanda smiled and quickly secured the weapon, slipping it into her own pocket. "New to the city, kid? Not much experience with door guardians either. Here's a little clue for you. Don't think murderous thoughts when you're about to pass one of them. It will make you very sick."

The woman glanced up, her eyes filled with hate, but she kept her mouth shut. Another tremor passed through her body and she was white as a sheet. "I suggest that you either think about something nice or go outside where you're out of range. Otherwise the building custodian is going to have to clean up a mes."

Her legs were unsteady but the younger woman managed to lurch through the doors and out onto the sidewalk. She crouched there for a while, hands on her knees, her color slowly returning. Wanda waited until she seemed steady on her feet. "If you're feeling up to it, we could go see Mr. Goodman now."

And they did.

CHAPTER TWELVE

Goodman was on his feet this time and opened the door himself. Wanda handed him the revolver. "This toy is a little advanced for that kid of yours." Goodman looked at the weapon as though he had never seen one before, then casually handed it to its owner.

"Put this away." He didn't look at her.

"Come sit down. Wilma will pour you a brandy." It was the first time Wanda had heard the younger woman's name. Goodman moved with an odd kind of grace and had settled gingerly into a chair by the time Wanda brought the drink. "Let me give you some free advice. Do not grow old and infirm." His long sigh hinted at pain.

"You wanted to talk to me."

"I always enjoy a spirited conversation."

"About the gargoyle."

"Ahh, directly to the point. Very well, I shall not keep you in suspense any longer. Let me ask you, have you ever heard of the Esoteric Order of Thule?"

"It's a rock band, isn't it?"

"Very droll. No, it's a secret society founded in Carpathia during the early 16th Century. They dabbled with a variety of magics with limited success. They were unfortunately not a particularly talented lot. Their efforts at necromancy were pitiful, their book of spells was less complete than what you might today find in any good library, and their astrologers were so imprecise that their advice was worthless."

"Sounds like the current city administration."

"Yes, I imagine so. They only lasted a few decades and are largely forgotten, but they did number among themselves one man of genius, George Bocskai. Bocskai is a bit of an enigma. We know very little about him other than his Transylvanian nationality. He never married and there is no record of his parentage. Although he is listed as a founding member of the Order, he never held any office within the organization. It appears that he rarely left his home, which was attached to a former lumbermill. Although he lived in a rather humble fashion, he paid for everything he needed with gold. Not coins, mind you, but lumps of gold of various sizes and shapes."

Wanda suppressed a groan. "This isn't another story about the man who could turn lead to stone, is it?"

Goodman had been slowly pacing back and forth, but he stopped. "Even the wildest stories have a basis in truth. Bocksai was indeed an alchemist and it seems very likely that he did discover the secret of transmutation."

"Then why didn't he manufacture enough to make himself rich and famous?"

"But that is the very last thing he would do. Tell me, why is gold of such great value?"

"Because of its scarcity." As soon as she spoke, Wanda began to anticipate what Goodman would say next. It was one of the more popular explanations employed in the transmutation myth. "I know. If it was possible to make gold out of dross, it would lose its value. I read *The Sword of the Rings* when I was a kid. Did you invite me up here to tell me fairy tales?"

"I have neither the time nor the resources at hand to prove to you what I believe to be true. I respect your skepticism, but it is irrelevant. I, as well as certain other parties, believe that Bocksai did indeed discover the secret, and used it only to satisfy his personal needs during his lifetime. That makes the gargoyle valuable to us. If we are fools, that's none of your concern. I will still pay handsomely to gain my objective."

"So how does the gargoyle come into this? Is it made of gold?" But Bridges had said she could easily throw the statue across a room. There had to be a different explanation.

"The gargoyle itself is virtually worthless except as a curiosity. But it contains the secret to transmutation. Bocksai died without revealing it, but he would not allow the knowledge he had acquired to disappear utterly. During the last years of his life, he became alienated from his former associates and decamped to the island of Malta, where he became a virtual hermit. He was sufficiently egotistic to wish his discovery to survive his death but sufficiently paranoid not to make the path to this knowledge well known. In Malta he created the statue as the vessel by means of which the secret could be passed on to whoever possessed both the gargoyle and the knowledge of its real purpose."

"So there's something hidden inside it?"

Goodman shrugged. "Perhaps. I don't know the nature of the key. The formula might be engraved on the exterior in some fashion, disguised of course. But your suggestion is the most likely explanation."

"Which means it's the key to infinite wealth."

"Not infinite. Remember, scarcity is what makes gold valuable. But it would certainly enable its possessor to life whatever style of life he or she aspired to."

"Okay, let's say I accept that story. How do you know this is the right gargoyle? It's been five hundred years since it was made."

"Would you care to see a picture of it?" Without waiting for an answer, Goodman moved to an ornate table in one corner of the room, opened a drawer, and extracted a manila folder. Wanda accepted it without rising. There were half a dozen photographs, all black and white, showing the gargoyle from various angles. It was very much as Bridges had described.

"Looks like a gargoyle to me."

"Take note of its forehead."

Wanda looked closely. "There are scratches of some kind."

"Runes. Almost obliterated, but still legible. The last one is an invented symbol which Bocksai used as his personal signet."

"That doesn't mean it isn't a copy, or an outright fake."

"This particularly gargoyle was cast in the year 1596. Bocksai died early in 1597."

"What did you do? Have it carbon dated?"

"It was tested by a Spell of Origin."

"Never heard of it."

"That's not surprising. They're very rare, and expensive. Only a Master Diviner can perform the spell, and not all of them."

"So how did you get involved?"

Goodman poured them both another brandy. "I was for a time informal partners with a man named Charon, who operated out of Athens. Charon performed a useful but not entirely legitimate service. He brought buyers and sellers together in an informal fashion for a commission. Much of his business was entirely above board but he sometimes offered his services to individuals who preferred not to make their transactions public."

"He was a fence."

"Among other things. Three years ago he showed me several items that he had acquired from one of his regulars, who unfortunately had recently been killed during an altercation with the Sicilian gendarmerie. Most of them had been acquired from a museum in Bratislava. These items had never been put on display and the museum was in fact still ignorant that they had been abstracted from one of their warehouses. Charon wished to dispose of the items before their absence was discovered and he asked me to take photographs – the ones you are holding were among them – to certain prospective buyers. One of those buyers expressed such intense interest in the gargoyle that it piqued my curiosity and I did some research of my own. I was, I confess, just as skeptical as you are when I discovered the stories about Bocksai, but I convinced Charon to invest in a Spell of Origin. When he telephoned me with the results, I offered to purchase the gargoyle myself. It took a few days to accumulate the necessary cash – Charon did not accept any other form of payment – but when I arrived I found my old friend lying dead, his skull crushed, at the foot of the stairs to his secret storeroom. The gargoyle, needless to say, was gone."

"Your prospective buyer acted first."

"Possibly, but I had shown the photographs to half a dozen people. It could have been any of them. I have been searching for the gargoyle ever since."

"So the real owner is some museum in Eastern Europe."

"Not necessarily. There was a reason why that particular lot of items was not publicly displayed. They had been stolen by parties unknown from a now extinct noble family in Bukovina. In a sense, there is no longer a proper owner. I have as good a claim as any."

"If Miss Bridges has possession, her claim seems a bit stronger to me."

"Miss Bridges was acting as my agent. Had I not employed her, she would never have known of its existence and she still does not know its actual value. Nor has she the knowledge to make use of its potential." Goodman's good humor was evaporating. "I will see that you are both amply rewarded for your trouble. As you can see, I have no reason to be parsimonious."

"It seems to me that you're getting ahead of yourself. Until you obtain the gargoyle, and discover how to make use of it, if it is the genuine article, you're limited to your current means. How much of a reward are you willing to provide upon delivery?"

Goodman's face hardened. "I am not a poor man, Miss Coyne, but naturally I would expect your patience in this matter. I would have no reason to cheat you."

"But you might be wrong about the gargoyle."

"Perhaps, but what have you to lose? And I can give you ten thousand dollars as a deposit immediately upon receipt. You will be that far ahead even if I prove to be a complete fool."

"Good point."

"So if you'll just tell me when you will make the delivery, I will arrange for the funds to be here. I assume there will be no problem acquiring it from Miss Bridges. Do you know where she is keeping it?"

"Not exactly."

Goodman pursed his lips. "I am very disappointed in you, Miss Coyne. You led me to believe that you knew its whereabouts already."

"Cool down, Goodman. I know how to get it from her."

"And when will you do so?"

"When I think the time is right." She decided that she had to give him something. "Two days from now. Is that long enough for you to get the cash?"

"It's more than ample. I assume I can entrust Miss Bridges' share to you as well. She was promised two thousand. Unless you would prefer that I deal directly with her."

"No, I can take care of it. Miss Bridges is tucked away somewhere safe for the duration."

Goodman smiled, his good humor restored. "Yes, I rather thought you would take that precaution. And it might cause friction if she were to learn more about our transaction. It is a pleasure dealing with someone who acts so professionally, if I may say so."

Wanda stood up then, and immediately regretted it. She'd begun to feel strange during the last few seconds and wanted to end the interview quickly, but she swayed and had to put a hand on the arm of the chair to keep from falling. The room was starting to spin and she would have thought she'd been drugged except that the talisman hanging around her neck was inert, so whatever it was hadn't been in the brandy.

Goodman was staring at her intently, but suddenly glanced to one side. Wanda managed to follow his eyes, but only with difficulty, and saw Wanda step toward her. She was holding something in one hand that glowed softly. The cool blue light seemed to reach out toward Wanda, inviting her to step into the glow, and she felt the will to resist seeping away. At the last moment she tried to turn away and stagger to the door, but she only managed a couple of steps before Wilma darted around in front of her, still holding the blue light and this time Wanda couldn't turn her eyes away. She was unconscious before she hit the floor.

When Wanda opened her eyes, the first thing she saw was the pattern of the rug in Goodman's suite. She started to get up and her head threatened to split wide open, so she took her time. Once she'd made it to her knees, she checked herself for hidden injuries and found nothing worse than a few bumps and scratches. The rooms felt and sounded empty but she checked them anyway. On the table near where she'd been lying she found a sleep globe, its glow now barely visible. She stayed out of range anyway. A quick search of the rooms turned up nothing but clothing, a handful of books on the esoteric arts, and odds and ends of no significance. She poured herself a brandy, but it made her sleepy again and she didn't finish it.

She let herself out and didn't lock the door behind her.

CHAPTER THIRTEEN

By the time she reached her office, her head felt normal but she was still tired. The sleep globe did not induce true sleep even though she had discovered that she'd been unconscious for six hours. Perry was in the office when she arrived, but he was obviously tidying up in preparation of calling it a day. "Any luck finding Miss Bridges?"

"I don't do my best work when I'm unconscious." She gave him a quick summary of her visit to Goodman.

Perry was righteously angry on her behalf. "Please tell me we're not taking him on as a client."

"I'm not sure what he is just yet. Can you take some notes for me? I have something I want you to check out." She repeated Goodman's story about the gargoyle in considerable detail while Perry jotted down the information. "It's too late today, but tomorrow morning I want you to stop by the Arcanium and talk to Professor Karruthers. I'd like to know what he makes of all this. I lean toward Goodman being a nutcase, but even delusions usually have some basis in reality." She yawned. "I'm going home, take some aspirin and a numbing potion, and going to bed."

"I found out something you might find interesting."

"Next week's winning lottery number?"

"Precognition is not among my many talents."

"They're shielded from precogs anyway. What have you got?"

"Gladys Willett's wedding announcement."

"She's getting married again? That must set a record."

"No, her first wedding. Her only wedding, to Nathan Willett."

"So what's interesting about it?"

Perry was enjoying himself. "I looked it up thinking I might be able to trace her background and I didn't need to be fey to guess the truth right away when I read the announcement. I made a couple of calls and confirmed it just before you got back."

"Confirmed what?"

"Gladys Willett was originally Gladys Taylor."

"As in Max Taylor?"

"He's her brother, though I don't know if anyone ever made the connection before. I tried to track down her family and found an obituary for the mother. Survived by two children, Gladys and Maxwell. Could be coincidence, but you don't like coincidences."

"No, I don't. Good work, Perry."

"Did you expect anything less? Oh, and you got a call from someone named Briana Dorr."

"What's she selling?"

"She's with the Office of Theurological Enforcement."

"What does she want with me? I'm not licensed for it, I don't do it, and I don't want to."

"She wouldn't say, but she was most anxious to speak with you." Perry retrieved a slip of paper from his desk. "Here's her number."

"I'll try to work her into my schedule. Tomorrow."

On her way home, Wanda stopped by the Tiara and checked Bridges' room, but there was nothing to indicate that she or anyone else had been there recently. She walked back to her apartment building, keeping an eye out for her shadow, but Wilma seemed to be otherwise occupied.

There was someone waiting for her in the lobby.

It was a woman wearing dark glasses and a veil, with her collar turned up and wearing gloves despite the warm weather. She was standing in the shadow of the staircase, clutching a shoulder bag tightly. Since the door guardian wasn't broadcasting alarm, Wanda wasn't worried but she was cautious.

"Can I help you?"

The other woman visibly shook herself before stepping out into the dim light. It was Diana Marks, so obviously under stress that it was a second before Wanda recognized her. "I have to talk to you, Miss Coyne."

Wanda sighed. She really did want to lie down and forget about Willett and Goodman and Bridges and all the rest, but obviously that wasn't going to happen yet. "All right. Come up to my apartment."

She made a pot of tea while her visitor tried unsuccessfully to relax. While it was brewing, Wanda took out the photograph of Willett and dropped it on the coffee table. Marks had lost her earlier self confidence and her next words suggested the reason. "Someone tried to kill me a little while ago."

"Have you called the police?"

"No. They're useless. They can't even figure out who shot Nathan Willett. They think I did it."

"I gather Captain Dandy has been out to see you again."

"No, it was someone named Masterton. He's a complete ass."

Wanda couldn't disagree. "Tell me what happened."

"I was jogging on the Common. I try to get out every morning when the weather's good. There was a homeless woman on the path, but there are always a few of them around and I didn't think anything of it until she stabbed me."

Wanda gave her the once over. "I don't see any blood."

"It was here." Marks held out her right hand. "She jabbed me in the palm as I ran by." There was a tiny red spot on her hand, almost invisible. "It hurt so badly that I stumbled and banged my knees. My hand went numb and turned purple and it started to spread up my arm."

"Medusa potion," said Wanda. "It only takes a drop and a tiny tear in the skin." She frowned. "But you should have died within minutes."

"I know. But Max makes me take this with me all the time." She fumbled inside her blouse and brought out an elaborate pendant with a thin gold chain that ran around the back of her neck. "He says most of my enemies are women and women prefer poison. This is supposed to neutralize the effect." She took a deep breath. "I guess it works. The transformation stopped before it reached my elbow and then reversed itself. By then the woman was gone, of course."

"What did she look like?"

"She looked like a homeless person. What do you think?"

"Tall, short, heavy? What color hair?"

"About average, I guess. She was bent over. She was wearing a shawl so I didn't really see her hair. Dark clothes, slacks rather than a skirt."

"Did she say anything?"

"Not a word."

"It might be happenstance. We do have some genuine crazies here in Boston." Wanda didn't believe it for a second. Medusa potions were expensive. Homeless people didn't buy them. And it would have been a pretty big coincidence. Wanda didn't like coincidences.

"So what do you want me to do about it?"

"Protect me. Find out who wants me dead and deal with them."

"Got any enemies?"

"Want a list? Use the Boston white pages. That's a start."

The teapot whistled and Wanda tended to it, then brought a tray with the tea, cups, sugar, and milk to the front room and set it down on the coffee table. Marks actually stirred herself to help, moving things out of the way to make enough room. When she picked up the magazine article, her eyes widened.

""Yes, that's your friend Nathan, the formerly up and coming businessman."

"That's not what I was looking at. I thought she'd gone out to the Coast. What's she doing with him?"

Wanda had that sudden insight that has nothing to do with magic. "Who are you talking about?"

"Selma Hairston. That's her sitting at the desk."

"You know her?"

"I certainly do. She worked for me for just over a year."

"She was your secretary?"

Marks laughed. "That's a good one. No, she was one of my most profitable escorts. Very much into bondage and some of the kinkier sidelines. Then one day she told me she was through with the trade and was going out to San Francisco to start a new life. I guess she never made it that far."

The gears in Wanda's head whirred and began to fall into place. "I don't suppose you remember who her clients were?"

"Some of them."

"Was our current deputy mayor one of them?"

"Myles? Definitely not. Myles is so conventional I don't think he even knows that the missionary position isn't the only possible combination. I had two or three girls that Myles liked and he wasn't interested in experimenting. I hear he's hinted that he might be getting married. I'm surprised it took him so long. Why the interest? You don't think he's involved in this somehow?"

"No, I don't think Myles Lewis is your problem and I don't think he killed Nathan Willett. But he definitely is involved."

"Are you going to tell me what's going on?

"No, no right now. But I think your problems will be over shortly. Do you have some place where you can stay for a day or two?"

"I have a little apartment no one knows about. Except Max, of course."

"Then go there, and watch the news."

Early the next morning, Wanda went back to Goodman's suite, but no one answered the door. She didn't know the security man on duty but a tenner got her the information he wanted. Goodman shared the suite with his "secretary", Wilma Fry, and his daughter, Athena. "The kid's good looking, nothing like her father. I saw her once in the dining room but not since then. She might have gone off on her own. Wouldn't blame her. The secretary's a jerk."

She walked to the Blue Hippogriff and found her contact sipping coffee in the security office. "Your boy is making the chambermaids happy. Didn't sleep here last night, didn't use the shower, and he hasn't had any messages."

Wanda considered her options. "I don't suppose you could look the other way while I took a look in his room?"

"My wife keeps telling me I need glasses. Sometimes I can't see things right in front of me. Hell, I wouldn't even notice if you borrowed the master key on that hook over there. I owe you one for the pickpocket."

"She wasn't really a pickpocket, Luke."

"I kinda knew that. Is she connected to Muscat?"

"In a way, I think, but maybe not directly."

Luke finished his coffee and pushed the cup away. "Does this have anything to do with Matt Bowman's murder?"

"I think so."

Luke stood up and grabbed the key. "Matt got me this job. Let's do it."

They stopped at the front desk where Luke told the clerk to ring Muscat's room if he came into the hotel before they were back. The clothing was cheaper than Goodman's and there were fewer other personal effects, but otherwise it was a repeat of the earlier search. Wanda picked up an ashtray and studied the contents. "He burned something here."

Luke joined him. "It's pretty far gone but I might be able to do something with it." He took an empty envelope with a hotel emblem in one corner from the desk of the writing table. Wanda gently tipped the ashtray so that the ashes slid inside. "Anything else you want to look at here."

She shook her head.

Back in the security office, Luke carefully placed the ashes into a pestle and sprinkled them with dust from a hotel sugar bowl. Then he covered the pestle with a piece of velvet, muttered a brief incantation, and then sat back and crossed his arms. "How long is this going to take?" Wanda had never actually sat through a reconstitution spell before.

"A couple of minutes. It was pretty well gone."

It took three minutes, but when Luke removed the cloth, a small piece of newsprint hovered just above the pestle. Carefully avoiding any physical contact, they both peered closely to read the revealed text. Luke copied the information to a piece of paper and had barely finished when the paper started to darken, then quickly returned to its ashen state, fell back into the pestle, and then silently exploded into ash.

"Looks like a list of port arrivals."

Each ship's name was followed by its port of origin. There were several from South America, but most were from Europe, two each from England and France, one from Portugal, one from Italy, and one from Split, Croatia. Wanda trusted her intuition and nodded toward the telephone, asking for permission to use it.

"Go ahead." Luke pushed his chair back.

Wanda called the Port Information Office and asked where the *The Dove* had docked, then noted down the pier number. Then she dialed Lieutenant Poorhouse's number and arranged to meet him for lunch. After struggling with her conscience, she dialed a third time and reached Briana Dorr's administrative assistant. The assistant could not tell Wanda why her boss wished to speak to her, but there was open time this afternoon. She never asked if Wanda was available, just assumed it, but by then Wanda's curiosity trumped her perverse streak and she agreed.

She thanked Luke and took a cab back to the office, arriving just as Perry was sitting down at his desk. "There you are. I have news."

"You saw the professor?"

"I did indeed."

"And he said?"

"He says that the story could very well be true, that there's nothing inconsistent with fact. On the other hand, there's no evidence supporting it either."

Wanda glanced at her watch. "Where does the time go? I have to run. Lunch date at the Portside."

"You should get a great view of the fire from there."

"What fire?"

Perry shrugged. "A big merchant ship in the harbor. There was smoke pouring out of it on both sides when I passed the waterfront."

Wanda wasn't psychic but sometimes she thought she might be. "You don't happen to know the name of the ship, do you?"

Perry shook his head. "Sorry. Too much smoke and I wasn't that interested."

But Wanda already had a pretty good idea that the ship was *The Dove*.

CHAPTER FOURTEEN

They sat on the porch overlooking the water, fortunately upwind of the still smoldering freighter. Poorhouse had ordered a heaped plate of Buffalo Style Cockatrice Wings but Wanda had opted for Kraken Chowder. They watched as the fireboats nuzzled around the stricken ship, pumping water through their hoses. *The Dove* was still afloat but Wanda doubted it would be salvageable. Most of the superstructure had collapsed into the holds.

"Has Dandy gotten over his disappointment that he couldn't lock me up the other night?"

"You shouldn't piss him off like that, Wanda. I know he's got a stiff one up the butt, but he's a straight shooter."

"Has the grief stricken widow come up with any more reasons why I should have killed Matt?"

Poorhouse shook his head wearily. "Dandy knows you didn't kill him, but he thinks you might have croaked Thursday to even the score. You know how it is with him. He keeps pushing in different directions until he thinks something's starting to move."

Wanda sensed something. "How does Dandy know I'm clean?"

Poorhouse looked uncomfortable. "We found salamander droppings in his room and there was a bag of charcoal. That's what they eat, you know."

"I know. So now I'm only the chief suspect in one murder instead of two."

"Not really. We found out a little about your Mr. Thursday. He's been a naughty boy. Worked for a rogue sorcerer up in Albany for a while but he tried to steal from his boss and got caught at it. He was smart enough to ask the Enchanter's League for sanctuary but ended up spending two years locked up in their safe house until his boss was finally brought down. After that he ran numbers and dope for one of the local gangs in Pittsburgh, but he crossed someone there too and went out to the West Coast for a few years. He kept a low profile there until he was caught with a Hand of Glory in the trunk of his car. Turned state's evidence and got a reduced sentence, which he served in Tennessee because his lawyer claimed he'd never survive a term in a prison near the Nostradamus Gang territory. They almost got him there, twice, and he was badly scarred on the back and shoulders by a blistering curse that got smuggled in past the wards."

"Popular guy."

""But not a very smart one. When he got out, he moved to Providence where he is suspected of selling love spells to minors. He was given the option of taking a new identity but declined. I guess he figured he wasn't a big enough annoyance that anyone would bother coming after him. Obviously he was wrong. Too bad they didn't show up a little earlier. Your partner might still be alive."

"So who do you think did it? Sounds like there are lots of candidates."

"We did a routine scrying but that almost never works. Asked around, found a couple of visiting heavies, one from San Francisco, one from Albany. We're looking at them."

"What about Joe Muscat? I assume you checked him out."

Poorhouse raised and lowered his shoulders. "His aura smells bad but we can't find anything specific in his record. We tried to convince him that it was in his best interest to cooperate but he shut up pretty quick and wouldn't talk."

"All night and you didn't get anything out of him?"

Poorhouse looked puzzled. "What do you mean, all night? We kept him about an hour but when it was obvious he wasn't going to talk we cut him loose."

So where had Muscat been during the interim? Wanda didn't say much for the rest of the meal, and she covered the check for both of them. "I have to run. Got an appointment with someone named Briana Dorr."

Poorhouse looked suddenly distressed. "What's the Dormouse want from you?"

"I don't know. A cup of tea maybe. What do you know about her?"

"She's a tough one. Doesn't look it but she's one of the big guns." He looked uncomfortable. "Say, you wouldn't mind not mentioning this little get together, would you?"

"Discretion is my middle name."

"You said you had something for me."

"I do. How would you like to wind up the Willett case?"

"I'm not on that team."

"No, but Dandy is and you work for Dandy most of the time. And Dandy doesn't like Masterton. So if you were to give Dandy the solution so he could stick it to Masterton, Dandy would owe you one, right?"

Poorhouse looked interested. "I'm listening."

She took out the magazine photo and showed it to him. "It turns out Miss Llewellyn here was formerly known as Selma Hairston. I'm not sure which is her real name or if they're both fake. Selma was for a time a high priced prostitute working for Diana Marks."

Poorhouse gave a little whistle. "And her boss was paying Marks for inside information about the indiscretions of certain prominent officials."

Wanda nodded. "But that wasn't why he was killed. Hairston was afraid that somewhere along the line her true identity would come out."

"Embarrassing. It would probably have cost her job. But that's a pretty thin excuse for murdering your boss. Why didn't she go after Marks if she was that desperate?"

"She would have eventually but she only found out about the deal the day Willett was killed. Marks left town that night, remember? She wasn't around to be targeted until the following afternoon."

"It's still a pretty thin motive."

"I haven't told you the motive yet. Miss Hairston, now Miss Llewellyn, was engaged to be married."

"I didn't know that."

"She's wearing an engagement ring, but men don't pay attention to that sort of thing. And the more important part wasn't visible – the name of her fiancé."

"Who is?"

"If I'm right, it's Myles Lewis."

"The mayor's deputy?" Poorhouse looked surprised, then not so surprised. "Do you think he was involved?"

Wanda shook her head. "I don't think Lewis knows about Hairston 's past. He was a client, but Marks says the two of them never got together. Lewis wants to be the next mayor. Even a hint of scandal and he'd drop her like a fire elemental."

Poorhouse was thoughtful for a few seconds. "This is good stuff. I think we can go to a judge with it and compel a directed scrying. Unless Hairston 's an unregistered sorceress, she won't be able to keep her secret."

Wanda glanced at her watch. "Glad to be of help, but I have to run. Use the information fast. I think Hairston has a short fuse."

Briana Dorr's office was at the end of a nondescript corridor in the wing of city hall unofficially devoted to problems involving the use of magic. She greeted Wanda with professional warmth but nodded to her secretary, who immediately closed her eyes to link to the departmental psi circuit. "Make yourself comfortable, Miss Coyne. One of my associates will be joining us."

Wanda found herself in a neat office whose decorations included not one object obviously related to the occult, which suggested exactly the opposite. Dorr, a tall, broad shouldered woman with her hair cut short, moved around behind the desk and sat down. "I understand that you and Captain Dandy have had some professional interaction recently?"

"And why are the police consulting with you about a run of the mill murder?"

"They aren't. But we have a staffer who reviews their logs and she flagged the case."

The door opened and a youngish man walked in. Dorr introduced him as Aaron Doyle. "He helps look into things that might have some relevance to our work here."

"So how does any of this involve me?"

"I understand your partner was killed by a salamander."

"That's what the forensics people say."

"Do you know who was responsible?"

Wanda shrugged. "If I did, I would have told Dandy. I'm a responsible citizen."

"No doubt." She stirred some papers on her desk as though consulting them, although her eyes never dropped. "The current theory is that the killer was a man named Lloyd Thursday."

"They mentioned that possibility to me."

"And Thursday himself was murdered within a few hours."

"They mentioned that as well."

"But they didn't find the salamander."

"No, they didn't. Maybe it was the salamander who shot him in the back."

Dorr sighed. "I'm not trying to ruffle your feathers, Coyne. Frankly, I don't care if you shot Thursday yourself. I'm after the salamander. We had a pretty good record here in the States up until a few years ago. Less than half a dozen incidents one year, mostly arson. There's been a slow but steady increase over the last ten years. Someone's breeding them and, for reasons I can't tell you, we're pretty sure the source is somewhere here in the Northeast. We need to find that source."

"Did you try the Yellow Pages?"

Dorr's lips thinned. "Aren't you overdoing the sarcasm a little?"

Wanda considered that, then nodded. "All right, how do you expect me to help you? I've told the police what little I know."

"Not quite everything. Who hired your partner to follow Thursday that night?"

"You think my client knocked off Thursday after he killed Bowman."

"I think it's possible."

"You know Thursday's background?" Dorr nodded. "Then you know that he had powerful, well heeled enemies, people who could easily afford a whole litter of salamanders. My client might be able to buy another bag of charcoal to keep them fed, but not much more."

"That you know of. Isn't it possible that your client has more resources than you realize?"

"The world is full of possibilities. I try to restrict what I believe to provable facts. Or at least strong probabilities."

"You know that withholding information in a capital case is a crime. It could cost you your license, or worse."

"Giving up my client without a good reason would have pretty much the same result. Look, Dorr, I understand what you want and if I was sitting on your side of the desk, I'd want the same thing. If I get a lead on anything to do with the salamander, I'll pass it on to you and the fine Captain Dandy. But until I have reason to believe otherwise, my first loyalty is to my client. Unless I have good reason to act otherwise, I'm going to do what I think is best. I wish you the best of luck with your investigation. But I have one of my own to conduct." She glanced at Doyle. "If we're done here, I have a busy schedule."

Doyle looked uncomfortable. Dorr looked unhappy. "I don't need to tell you that it's not wise to have enemies in this department, Coyne."

Wanda stood up. "No, you don't. I prefer to choose my enemies, but sometimes I don't always get what I want. None of us do. We have to live with that, don't we?"

Dorr was silent a moment. "We'll talk again.

CHAPTER FIFTEEN

Wanda returned to her office where Perry told her that he hadn't heard from Bridges or Goodman or Muscat or even the police. "She could be anywhere by now," Perry said unhelpfully. "She might have left the city right after she dumped me. We don't even have a picture of her to show around. Maybe we should buy one of those aura sensitive cameras for the office?"

Wanda shook her head. "No, I doubt very much that she skipped town. I'm pretty sure she went out to *The Dove*."

Perry looked puzzled. "Isn't that the ship that burned?" His expression turned to alarm. "You don't think she's dead, do you? I haven't heard anything about them finding bodies in the wreckage."

"They're still looking, but no, I don't think she's dead. And I think our other client, Mr. Muscat, may have gone there as well."

As if by magic, the phone rang. Perry mumbled into it, then handed the receiver to Wanda. "It's someone named Luke."

Joe Muscat had returned to his room at long last. She thanked Luke for the tip, told Perry to mind the shop, and tried to flag down a cab. Naturally they were particularly scarce when she was in a hurry and she finally decided to walk to the Hippogriff. Luke was waiting for her in the lobby.

"You just missed him."

"Off again?" She let her frustration show.

"Worse. Checked out with no forwarding address." Luke shook his head. "But I did note the number of the cab he took." He handed her a slip of paper.

"Thanks. I owe you." She pocketed the paper and stepped outside. There were six cabs waiting for fares. Wanda almost walked past them but at the last minute she had an idea. She slipped into the first one in the rank. "Take me to the waterfront."

"Anywhere in particular?"

"As close as you can get to the pier where that ship burned."

The dock was cordoned off but there was enough confusion caused by investigators, remediation teams, and rubberneckers that Wanda was able to talk to some people who shouldn't have talked but took her cash as well as several others who just liked to hear the sound of their voices. Wanda described Bridges and the clothes she had been wearing when she stranded Perry and a few people remembered, or thought they remembered, or pretended that they remembered seeing her. She'd been asking questions about *The Dove* and its captain, Jacobs. A burly longshoreman said she'd tried to go aboard just after noon but had been refused. "She was asking after Jacobs because they told her he was ashore someplace, but he didn't come back until late in the afternoon. I saw her sitting out on the dock throwing bread to the gulls once before that, but I don't remember what time it was."

It turned out that Jacobs was a regular at one of the local bars. A waitress told her that he and another man with a jagged scar on his forehead had stopped in for a drink that afternoon and that some woman had come in and talked to him. "I don't remember what she looked like, but she was youngish. I brought them one round and then some other people came in and right after that they all left together right after that."

"What did the newcomers look like?"

"I really don't know. One of them was very tall and skinny and he walked kind of funny, but I don't remember much about the other two. One was a guy with no fashion sense; the other wasn't much more than a girl."

Wanda described Joe Muscat and Wilma Fry. "That could be them, I guess. Look, I got customers waiting on me. It's supposed to be the other way around."

Wanda used the public phone to call Poorhouse, who was at his desk for a change.

"What can you tell me about the harbor fire?"

"Not much. Lockesley had the case until this morning."

"What happened this morning?"

"Your buddy Dorr claimed jurisdiction."

"How did she manage that?" But Wanda already had an inkling.

"Apparently the fire department found evidence the fire was started by a salamander."

"What did Lockesley have before they cut him out?"

"Next to nothing. Nobody saw anything until the smoke started pouring out of one of the forward hold. It spread pretty quickly though so Lockesley suspected it was set. We were combing through the wreckage and looking for the captain when the call came to drop it and turn over everything we had."

"Hass the captain turned up yet?"

"You'd have to ask Dorr about that."

Wanda thanked him and hung up.

It was getting toward the end of the day when she finally got back to the office. Perry had nothing for her and she wasn't sure where to look next. She didn't know anybody in Dorr's organization so she couldn't probe there and she still had no idea where Bridges had gone to ground. It appeared that there had been some sort of reconciliation among the contestants for the gargoyle, but the possibility that the fire aboard *The Dove* had been started by a salamander was intriguing. Was it meant to conceal something, or might it have been an accident? Salamanders were notoriously difficult to manage except by experienced trainers.

She was tired, mentally and physically, so after checking the mail she went back to the outer office to send Perry home early. Before she could speak, the outer door opened and a heavyset man walked in. No, that was wrong. He staggered in. Wanda recoiled a step immediately when she recognized the sorcerer's cloak wrapped around his body, but then she saw his face, distorted into a mask of pain, and his next step was tentative. He was carrying a good sized package, clutched tightly against his body, but it seemed to slip from his fingers and hit the floor with a dull thud. Then his knees folded involuntarily and without a word he collapsed to the floor.

Wanda overcame her reluctance and knelt over the man. His cloak had fallen open and she could see something darker beneath it. Her nose told her it was blood even before she lifted the edge of the cloak away to expose a gaping wound in the man's chest. It was tacky to the touch but obviously well on its way to drying out. He was not breathing, probably hadn't for at least several minutes. There was a lightning jagged scar on his forehead. She glanced up but Perry had already gone to lock the door. He started toward the telephone but she shook her head. "He's past that. Not even a revenancer can bring back a sorcerer once he's gone. Their auras are too powerful." She spread the cloak further, forcing herself to examine the wound objectively.

Perry came back toward the dead man but kept his distance and his voice was shaking. "What happened to him?"

Wanda took a breath. "He took a bullet in the heart."

Perry shook his head. "But that would have killed him right away, wouldn't it?"

"One would think. He must have put himself under a powerful compulsion to make it here after he was dead." She forced herself to search the corpse, but the pockets in the cloak and pants were both empty. She stood up and retrieved the fallen package, set it down on Perry's desk. There was a smear of blood on one side. "Let's get this open."

Wanda had a pretty good idea what she was going to find, but at the same time it seemed too easy. She unwrapped it carefully in case there were any protective wards mixed with the plastic peanuts, but she didn't find any. Beneath it was a layer of bubblepack which she carefully unwrapped. Inside was the rather unremarkable statue of a gargoyle, exactly as Goodman had described it.

"Well curse me," she said softly. "Here it is."

Perry overcame his reluctance and came forward to look at their prize but was forestalled by the telephone. He grabbed the receiver. "Coyne Detective Agency. May I help you?" His eyes narrowed and Wanda felt her pulse quicken. She could almost hear the other voice on the line, a female voice that was cut short. Whoever it was had hung up.

"Who was that?"

"It was Miss Bridges." Perry seemed stunned. "She said she's in danger and wants you to come to the Imperial Hotel right away."

"What kind of danger?"

"I don't know. She hung up."

"Damn!" She thought furiously. "All right, this is what we'll do. Gather up all those peanuts and wrap them up with this." She handed Perry the gargoyle. "As soon as I'm gone, you call the police and tell them what happened, but don't mention the package. I'll take it with me."

"But what about you? They'll want to know where you are."

"Tell them that I got a call and rushed out without saying anything. Don't say more than you have to and don't volunteer anything. With any luck, as soon as they see what they've got here they'll call Dorr or one of her cronies and by the time they get jurisdiction sorted out, I might be back to pick up the ball."

Perry glanced back down at the corpse. "Do you know who he is? Or was?

Wanda shook her head. There were half a dozen sorcerers living in Boston and Wanda knew all of their faces from news stories or elsewhere, but the dead man was a stranger. "I don't think he's local. I'm pretty sure he was a passenger on *The Dove*. Are you okay?"

"Sure." His voice was shaking but they would expect that. "I'll be back as soon as I can."

Wanda stopped at a UPS store and had the gargoyle repackaged and shipped overnight to Perry Everdeen's address before heading over to the Imperial. Since she couldn't think of any viable alternative, she decided to rush headlong ahead, took the elevator, and pounded on the door to Goodman's suite. There was no answer so she took out her lock pick and went to work on the door. Since most burglars used admission spells to get into places they weren't supposed to be, the mechanics of actual physical locks had not progressed much in decades and it only took a few seconds before she heard the lock click and opened the door.

At first glance the suite appeared to be empty but once she was a few steps inside, she spotted someone sitting in a straight backed plush chair off to one side. Wanda flinched with surprise but the figure – a strikingly attractive young woman – gave no sign that she was aware of the intruder. In fact, she barely seemed to breathe and never blinked at all. Wanda came closer and saw that her eyes were focused on a green tinted crystal propped up on the tiny end table in front of her.

Wanda had never seen her before, but she knew what the crystal was, or rather what it must be. She made a quick search of the other rooms without finding anything of interest, then returned with a towel, which she dropped over the crystal. The young woman immediately blinked, shook her head slightly, and then began to slip off the chair, her arms and legs limp. Wanda caught her before she hit the floor and helped her over to the couch. The girl's eyes were unfocused and she seemed unaware of her surroundings but she didn't resist.

Wanda poured two brandies and managed to get half of one of them down the girl's throat. She coughed and tossed her head, but her eyes cleared slightly and she made an effort to sit up. Wanda took the chair facing her and slowly sipped at her own drink.

It was obvious that the girl had recovered more quickly than she let on, but Wanda was content to let her think she was regaining some control of the situation. When she was certain that the confusion was feigned, she leaned forward.

"Who are you?"

"I might ask you the same question."

"Let me take a stab at it. You're Goodman's daughter."

All pretense immediately faded away. "Yes, I'm Athena. You know my father?"

"We've had some business together. Where is Miss Bridges?"

There was a pause and Wanda could almost read her mind. She was trying to decide whether or not to play dumb. The proposition lost. "Who's side are you on in all this?"

"I don't even know who the sides are yet. Where is she? Where's your father?

"They're together. She's in danger. My father is a very determined man. He won't let anyone stand in his way when he wants something. Not even me."

"I've met him, remember. None of this is news to me. Is Bridges all right?"

"She was when they left, but I think he's planning to dispose of her once he decides he doesn't need her anymore."

"Where are they?"

Athena looked as though she wanted to say something, but she choked up and began to cough. Wanda poured her another brandy but she waved it off. "They used the crystal to implant a compulsion. I had to promise not to say anything to anyone about where they went."

Wanda closed her eyes and shook her head in frustration. As she did so, Athena stood up rather shakily and started across the room. "I'm okay. I need to do something." She crossed to the small desk, found a pen, and began writing on a sheet of hotel stationery. When she was done, she brought it to Wanda, then collapsed onto the couch.

There was an address written on the paper. Athena gave her a wry smile. "I promised not to say anything, but they didn't tell me I couldn't write something. You'd better hurry."

"You'll be alright here?"

"As much as I ever am."

CHAPTER SIXTEEN

The address was in Newton, west of the city. It was one of the few times when Wanda wished she owned a car. She thought about it for a minute or two, then found a public phone kiosk and called an old friend who owed her a favor. She drank coffee at Starbucks until a red Nissan stopped in front, idling impatiently.

"Thanks for coming, Timmy." She slid in beside a slightly built man in his late twenties. Timmy had been a client, sort of, since she'd never taken any of his money. He'd been fingered for a liquor store robbery that he hadn't done, which wasn't to say that he hadn't actually ever held one up, and Wanda had found the real thief, who'd used a chameleon spell to disguise his appearance. Timmy owed her and he acknowledged it cheerfully.

"No problem. I wasn't doing nothing anyway."

"I need to get to Newton."

Timmy pulled away from the curb and accelerated through a yellow light. "How soon do we need to be there?"

"Don't get a ticket on my account."

Timmy was an excellent driver, a skill which Wanda had no doubt he marketed to some of the city's less savory characters. Traffic was a bit heavier than usual, but somehow he always managed to figure which lane was going to move faster and from time to time he chose side streets that Wanda hadn't even realized existed. They reached Hamsa Street at dusk and Wanda had Timmy let her out a block away from her destination. It was a residential neighborhood, but surprisingly quiet. She borrowed the flashlight he kept in the glove compartment. "Wait here for me."

"You're sure you'll be okay. I came prepared." Timmy showed her the handgun tucked into his pants, which she'd already spotted.

"I'm just taking a look see."

The house was dark and silent. Wanda walked around the grounds, which were well enough lit by the nearly full moon that she didn't need the flash. The back door was locked but not very well. Wanda didn't even need her pick to circumvent the lock and there were no paranormal defenses that she could detect. That didn't mean they weren't there, of course. A psychic dispatcher at Newton Police headquarters might already be sending an officer to investigate, but she didn't think so. The place felt abandoned.

Inside she used the flashlight, but discreetly so that it couldn't be seen from outside. There was furniture, most of it threadbare, but not a lot of it. There were two stories, seven rooms, and she checked them all. No one was home and she suspected no one had been home for a long time. The refrigerator was empty and unplugged. There were no linens on the beds. Disappointed, but not particularly surprised, she left the way she had come in and made her way back to the car.

"Find anything?"

She hated to dampen Timmy's enthusiasm, but she couldn't offer him much. "Sometimes when you find nothing, that's something."

He nodded as though she'd said something profound and started the engine.

Timmy dropped her off at home and she poured herself a drink, then called Perry's home number. "Did you find her, boss?"

"No. It was a wild goose chase. How did it go with the cops?"

"They took me downtown for a couple of hours. Captain Dandy isn't going to be sending you a birthday card this year. He kept talking about leaving the scene of crime and obstructing justice. I thought he was going to have a stroke right in front of me."

"Do they know who the dead man was?"

"If they did, they didn't tell me."

"I hope they weren't too hard on you."

"It's mostly you they're mad at. I just shrugged and told them you didn't tell me a lot. Which was pretty much true."

"I don't know that much myself."

"Dandy said he was going to have you arrested."

"He's bluffing. I'm sitting in my apartment and there wasn't even someone watching the building. And now I think I'm going to bed."

"There's one thing," Perry said quickly. "When we were leaving the office, I saw someone watching."

"Anyone we know?"

"Might be. From your description, I think it was the woman you said worked for Goodman."

"Interesting. Perry, I want you to do something for me."

"Sure, boss."

"If you see that young lady again, keep your distance and stay with other people."

"She didn't look that scary."

"It's not what she looks like that worries me. It's what's going on inside her head."

She had barely hung up the phone when the door imp opened its eyes. "You are about to have a visitor, a young woman."

Heedful of her own warning, Wanda retrieved a long bladed knife from the kitchen before approaching the door. She didn't keep firearms in her apartment. There was a sudden, almost frantic knocking on the door and Wanda opened it quickly, hoping to put her visitor off balance. She'd been expecting it to be Wilma Fry, but it wasn't. It was Faye Bridges.

"Close the door! She's right behind me!"

Wanda was about to do that very thing when a voice spoke from behind them. "Please leave it open. It would be most impolite to leave poor Wilma standing on the landing."

Goodman and Muscat stepped out of the darkened bedroom. Muscat held a firedrake in one hand and it was extended in Wanda's direction. She stepped away from the door as the imp spoke again, sounding put upon. "You are about to have a visitor, a young woman." Wilma appeared at the threshold. She was armed more conventionally with a small handgun.

"You may close the door now, Miss Coyne, but please do so gently. We don't want any unnecessary trouble, do we?"

"I suppose you want to deal about the gargoyle" Wanda steered Bridges over to the loveseat and pushed her down into it. The door guardian in the lobby should have picked up on the felonious thoughts of the intruders but obviously hadn't, which suggested that one of the pair had access to powerful magic. She would need to be cautious. "A simple invitation would have sufficed. You knew I planned to turn it over to you, for a suitable fee, of course."

"Ah, yes. Your fee." Goodman reached into his pocket and withdrew a roll of bills wrapped with a rubber band. He tossed it to Wanda, who caught it, then ostentatiously removed the rubber band and counted it.

"This isn't what we agreed to."

"Our previous negotiations were made on an equal footing. The balance of power has shifted since then." Goodman glanced at Muscat's firedrake. "I don't recommend that you attempt to reopen negotiations at this point."

"I take your point. But there are other matters we need to discuss before we can complete the deal."

"What matters might those be?" There was tension in Goodman's voice now. "I warn you, Miss Coyne, that no one here has the patience for another round of diversions."

"I'm just being practical. You're not looking at the whole picture here. Let's say I accept your offer and turn over the statue. That still leaves us with a couple of murders to account for. Three if the police don't agree that Thursday killed my partner."

"I assume you have a point to make."

"Sure. Isn't it obvious? We have to give them a plausible scenario for the killings, and that means we have to decide who pulled them off."

"The police don't know of my involvement in this." Goodman sounded smug, but Muscat narrowed his eyes and seemed about to say something. Wanda cut him off.

"They have your name, at least your assumed name. I gave it to them. Don't think that you're off the hook just because they haven't come around to see you yet."

Goodman's eyes narrowed. "I am disappointed in you, Miss Coyne. I thought your ethical code would prevent you from revealing our business to the authorities."

Wanda sat down besides Bridges and crossed her legs. "Well, you're not exactly a client, so confidentiality doesn't come into it. And survival trumps ethics anyway. But don't raise a sweat. There's a way to arrange things so the police lose interest."

"And that would be?"

"We give them the killer, or rather, someone they'll accept as the killer. They won't look too hard because they just want the case closed, so we don't have to fill in all the details. A rough sketch will do."

Goodman looked interested. "But where would we find this paragon of guilt?"

Wanda turned her head and looked meaningfully at Wilma. "She killed Thursday, didn't she? And who's to say she didn't use some illegal spell to burst the other guy's heart? Or even a real basilisk. Enough time has passed that there would be no basilisk fire residue on her hands. You don't have to have physical strength or even much of a brain to focus a spell and activate it."

Wilma said nothing but her posture became ever so slightly more alert.

Goodman smiled. "And what would prevent Wilma – assuming I was to go along with your outlandish scheme – from telling everything she knows to the police? That would hardly improve our situation."

"Well, naturally she'd have to be dead, and we'd have to keep her body on ice long enough that the forensics couldn't read her brain." She glanced at Wilma. "Assuming they could find it."

Wilma gave her a look that should have turned her to stone, but Goodman laughed. "What do you think of this idea, Wilma? Do you think Miss Coyne has a valid point?"

"I think she talks too much."

"But we should at least hear her out. The plan might have merits if someone else was cast in the part." He turned back to Wanda. "The police are very insistent upon having a motive. Why would Wilma, or another party acting in her stead, feel inclined to murder both Thursday and Hamut?"

Wanda registered the latter name, proof if she needed it that the Goodman knew the dead sorcerer.

"Hamut was smuggling salamanders into the country, wasn't he?"

Goodman didn't blink. "Possibly."

"What if Wilma here was working for him? They had some kind of falling out and the kid was smart enough to have a spell that could get through his defenses. We know she's not that bright, but if she's dead when the cops get to her, they won't."

"And Thursday?"

"Hamut ordered her to knock him off after he used a salamander to kill my partner. The cops were on Thursday's tail and would have picked him up within hours if he hadn't been killed. He might have talked and endangered the entire operation."

"Ingenious, I admit. But I'm afraid I'm not ready to sacrifice Wilma. She has been very loyal to me and I think of her as a daughter." A hint of a frown chased itself across Goodman's face. "More than a daughter in some ways. I don't say there is no merit in your proposal, but I'm afraid it just won't do."

"Alright," said Wanda. "Then what about him?" She looked pointedly at Muscat, who immediately began to squirm.

"And how would you fit Mr. Muscat into your mosaic?"

"Well, I admit he's not as good a fit, but he could still be Hamut's partner, so he'd have the same motive for knocking off Thursday. And the police already know he's fond of arcane weaponry, so he works as Hamut's killer as well. We'd still have to make sure the cops didn't get him until he was all the way dead, but that's true no matter who we pick. I'd still go for the girl, but it's not a deal breaker."

Muscat had less self control than Wilma. He stepped forward, his hand shaking, face working furiously for a few second before he could speak. "Why don't we cast you in the part, Coyne? You could have knocked off Thursday to avenge your partner, and maybe you found out that he was following orders from the sorcerer so you went after him as well. Lured him to your office and killed him there."

"Don't blow your top, Muscat. We're just talking possibilities here." Wanda turned to look at Bridges, who was cowering at her end of the love seat. "We could even cast this young lady in the part if we wanted to. She hired us because she was afraid of Thursday and she decided to get him before he did the same to her. We've have to find a motive for Hamut, but I'm sure among the three of us we could come up with something."

But Muscat wasn't so easily diverted. "What makes you think you're calling the shots here? The way I see it, we're the ones who get to decide what happens next."

Wanda nodded. "Up to a point. But that point is the stickler because I'm still the only one here who knows where the gargoyle is. Trust me, gentlemen. You can search this apartment and my office to your heart's content and you will find nothing that will lead you to its present location." Unless, she thought to yourself, you are bright enough to search Perry's house, and dumb enough not to do it until after the package arrives.

"There are spells of compulsion," suggested Goodman.

"But they're not very reliable, are they? What's the failure rate, around fifty percent?"

"There are also physical means of persuasion that we could use."

"You could try."

There was a long, uncomfortable silence. Then Goodman glanced at Wilma. "Watch them." He gestured to Muscat and the two retreated into Wanda's bedroom.

Wanda glanced up at Wilma. "They're buying my plan, kid. They'll come back and one of them'll get the drop on you or maybe just kill you outright. Then we stash your body someplace for long enough to empty your brain so the cops won't find anything when your body turns up, maybe with a written confession to help them along."

"Shut up."

"Hey, I'm just trying to lend a hand. You could slip out the door and disappear. I won't try to stop you and I don't think either of them is up to chasing you down. Even you should be smart enough to be able to stay ahead of them."

Wilma had been doing a quiet boil for some time but Wanda had finally provoked her enough to spark an unwise response. She raised her weapon and started toward the love seat, murder in her eyes. Wanda had a moment to wonder if she'd miscalculated but just then Muscat reappeared. His eyes widened and he instinctively raised the hand holding the firedrake. Wilma caught the motion out of the corner of her eye, interpreted it as a threat, and spun awkwardly to bring her weapon to bear.

Wanda propelled herself off the couch and smashed her shoulder into Wilma's side. The younger woman wasn't much more than a hundred pounds and grunted with pain as she slammed into the wall. Muscat triggered the firedrake, although it's possible even he didn't know which woman was his target, and a plume of acidic fluid narrowly missed Wanda's head and splattered, hissing, against the far wall. She ignored it and went for the fallen handgun.

Wilma regained her balance and lunged toward the same spot and their heads cracked together. Wanda winced, but her hand found the weapon and pulled it in. Wilma hit the floor limply, made one brief effort to rise, then fell back unconscious. Goodman had emerged as well and Wanda swiveled to cover both of them with Wilma's gun. "Let's put the firedrake down on the coffee table, shall we?"

Muscat raised the artifact uncertainly.

"Come on, Muscat. You and I both know it takes a while to revitalize itself. Now put it down."

Reluctantly, Muscat complied. Goodman looked unworried, but unhappy. "You're a resourceful woman, Miss Coyne. I salute you."

"Sorry, that doesn't make my heart go pitter patter." She glanced at Wilma, still unconscious on the floor. "So what did you decide in there about my plan?"

Goodman sighed. "Wilma has been with me for two years. I have never had cause to complain of her loyalty."

"So buy yourself a dog."

"It may be hard for you to believe this, but I do have a sense of ethics."

"You're right. It's hard for me to believe."

Goodman ignored her. "But in this case, expediency trumps sentiment, I'm afraid. Wilma is valuable but not beyond replacement."

"So we give her to the cops?"

"Unless you have a more promising proposal."

CHAPTER SEVENTEEN

Muscat had some second thoughts about giving up Wilma, but he let himself be talked out of them without much difficulty. Goodman seemed genuinely saddened by the necessity but resigned to it. Bridges never said a word and stayed on the loveseat. Wilma did not regain consciousness even when Goodman put a pillow under her head and arranged her splayed limbs more comfortably.

"And our transaction will take place today," prompted Goodman at last.

Wanda nodded, then realized she no longer held the roll of bills. A quick glance back toward the loveseat was unproductive and she smiled. "Miss Bridges is holding the money for me."

Bridges was not as disoriented as she pretended. Her head snapped up defiantly, but she nodded. "Yes, I picked it up when you dropped it. I was keeping it safe."

Goodman dismissed the money. "I must ask that you carry out our plan by humane means."

Wanda nodded. "She won't feel a thing."

"I accept your promise. You will, of course, wait until we have had time to leave Boston before setting things in motion."

"She'll have to sit for at least twenty-four hours to be sure the aura is completely dispersed. I can wait longer if necessary."

"No, that should be ample time. We will leave almost immediately upon receiving the gargoyle."

"I can arrange to have it delivered to your hotel room."

"You have me at a disadvantage already, Miss Coyne. Surely you don't expect me to let you out of my sight until I have received what I have paid for."

"No, of course not. Anyway I'll need more information from you if I'm going to make the story work."

Goodman was immediately wary. "What kind of information?"

"I assume that Wilma did kill Thursday so that should be fairly easy to sell. But I need to know more about Hamut and his operation."

"I don't see the necessity at all. In fact, it might raise questions if you knew more than you should. I can tell you that the bullets that killed Thursday will match the markings in that weapon you just took from Wilma. That should be enough to satisfy the police."

"If I'm going to make the story stick, I need to know if something is going to turn up that contradicts my version. If I say that Wilma was acting on Hamut's instructions and it turns out there was no way they could have communicated at the right time, our plans falls apart. So I need to know the real reason Wilma eliminated him."

Goodman sighed. "Thursday and Miss Bridges were working for a competing interest. It seemed only logical to discourage them in the most efficient way possible."

"And Hamut?"

For a second she thought Goodman wouldn't answer, but then the will to resist seemed to desert him. "Mr. Hamut was the competing interest in question. He was unwise enough to intervene personally and the opportunity was too appealing to overlook."

"So Hamut hired Bridges and Thursday, and Thursday doublecrossed him?"

"As far as I know, Thursday's only perfidy involved Miss Bridges, whose share of the reward he hoped to keep to himself."

"Then Thursday did have the gargoyle?"

"Such I believe to be the case."

"Then why didn't he turn it over to Hamut?"

"Perhaps he was negotiating the price. Perhaps he didn't have time. Hamut had only just arrived on *The Dove*, you see."

"If you thought that was the case, why didn't you contact Thursday and try to outbid Hamut?"

"Oh, I did. Thursday was clearly tempted, but he was afraid of his employer. It is not a good idea to cross a sorcerer, even a defrocked sorcerer. I can't entirely blame him, but I could not allow the gargoyle to be delivered to Hamut. It would have been much more difficult to acquire once it was in his possession. Wilma suggested a solution that would at least give us some time to seek an alternate outcome and I authorized her to act."

"And Hamut?"

"That was a crime of opportunity. Mr. Muscat here is a freelancer. He would have happily sold the gargoyle either to myself or Hamut, but once he became convinced that it was in Thursday's possession, he realized he was in danger of losing any chance of a reward. He approached me and suggested an arrangement; he had information that I lacked. Although I knew of Hamut's interest, I believed that he was still in Europe. Joe new about Hamut's clandestine import business via *The Dove* and was aware of its arrival in Boston."

Muscat stirred uncomfortably. "I had done business with him in the past."

Goodman ignored the interruption. "Bridges also knew that Hamut was aboard *The Dove* and she went to report her progress, or lack thereof, but Hamut had gone ashore. She found Captain Jacobs instead, as did we, but the captain knew – or admitting knowing – very little about his passenger. He did, however, mention that Hamut had received a parcel by special delivery the previous evening and as far as he knew, it was still aboard the ship. We prevailed upon him to invite us aboard on the pretext that we would wait for Hamut to return, but once there we were shockingly bad guests and made him our prisoner while we searched for the package. To no avail, although we did find a hidden room in the hold which contained six small cages. You can guess what was in them."

"Salamanders."

Goodman nodded. "Unfortunately, there was some kind of magical ward that we violated and the salamanders became extremely agitated. We barely escaped the room before the conflagration began. I believe the ward also warned Hamut, wherever he was at the time, because he arrived just as things aboard the ship were becoming lively. He retrieved the package from one of the lifeboats. It must have been rendered invisible or otherwise transformed because we had looked there earlier. He was almost certainly aware of our presence aboard but he was overconfident. The firedrake didn't worry him at all but he was unprepared for a more mundane attack. He seemed quite surprised when Wilma shot him."

"But he got away."

"As we both know, he did indeed. He quite literally walked across the harbor to the far side, concealed himself somehow and then – for reasons I do not entirely understand – eventually went to your office to die. Miss Bridges had earlier communicated to him her plan to approach you in this matter, but I cannot otherwise account for his arrival at your office. I had been listening to police broadcasts hoping to hear something about a shooting victim and much to my surprise, your name came up again. We prevailed upon Miss Bridges to lure you away and Wilma made an effort to arrive before the police, but she was unsuccessful. In any case, you have the gargoyle, for which I have paid you a knightly if not princely sum, and there are no other bidders to whom you might turn."

Wilma stirred and mumbled something incoherent. Wanda shifted position so that she could cover everyone in the room with the handgun, including Bridges. "All right, this is how we're going to handle this. I can't get the statue until tomorrow so there's no point to us sitting around looking at one another all night."

Goodman looked unhappy. "You will understand if I feel that it would not be in my best interests to leave you to your own devices just now."

Wanda nodded. "Unfortunately for you, I have all the weapons at the moment. But I'm not suggesting that you leave. I think you should all stay right here. I have a few things to do tonight and tomorrow I'll retrieve the parcel and bring it here. Then we make the final arrangements for Wilma there and complete the deal."

Goodman was still frowning. "Miss Fry will recover soon. I assume that you will leave us a weapon to ensure her cooperation."

Wanda shook her head. "You'll have to tie her up."

"I'm coming with you," said Bridges.

"Afraid not, kid. You wait with the rest of them."

Bridges looked as though she was going to argue, but she subsided after a moment. "She will leave as soon as you're gone," suggested Goodman.

"I imagine the two of you will be able to dissuade her. Tie her up if you have to."

"And what's to prevent Mr. Muscat or myself leaving and returning with another weapon during your absence?"

"I thought of that. How did you get past the door guardian in the lobby?"

Goodman was positively squirming. "I used a masking spell. Expensive but effective."

"Look, just because I'm not licensed to use magic doesn't mean I don't know how it works. Spells only work against people or material objects because there has to be a physical component to any instance of magic. The door guardian is metaphysical so you could only fool it by using an enchantment seated in a physical object."

Goodman didn't argue, just looked away as though he'd lost interest.

"So hand it over."

With a sigh, Goodman reached into a pocket and pulled out a ruby red amulet on a golden chain. "This cost me a great deal of money, Miss Coyne. I'll want it back when we have completed our business together."

Wanda accepted the amulet thoughtfully. "I'm going to invoke the guardian on the way out. If this is the real thing, it won't acknowledge my existence."

Goodman sighed again, more deeply this time. "I seem to be making a habit of underestimating you." He retrieved another object, this one resembling an oversized pearl. "If I might have the euphorium back? It eases the pain in my spine."

Wanda made the exchange.

At first light, she found a cab and gave the driver Perry's address. Perry had hidden the package in the hall closet. When Wanda asked for it, he retrieved it promptly. "I told Julia it was a present for our anniversary. Now I have to be sure to get her something the right size."

"She probably knows you were lying."

"Yeah, she probably does. But she'll make me play the game to the end."

"I'm getting near an endgame myself."

Wanda still wasn't sure how everything was going to play out but instinct told her that it was time to lay the last cards on the table. She returned to her apartment building and slipped the charm into her mailbox so that the door guardian would recognize her. It had nothing to tell her. She retrieved the charm and went upstairs.

If it hadn't been for the litter of dirty coffee cups, Wanda might have thought that no one had moved since she'd left them the previous evening. Bridges looked a little the worse for wear with droopy eyelids and Goodman's suit was looking a bit crumpled around the edges. Wilma Fry was awake, tied securely to a chair, and she gave Wanda a withering glance without saying a word. Muscat somehow managed to appear as dapper as ever, but his shoulders were slumped with fatigue and tension.

"What no rousing welcome?" Wanda held out the package so they could all see it. The change in atmosphere was tangible.

Wanda let Goodman take the package, which he placed reverently on the coffee table. Muscat brought a knife from the kitchen so that they could cut the cords. Goodman was visibly restraining himself, removing the packaging delicately even though he wanted to rip it off. Wanda retreated to one corner, trying to watch everyone at once. Only Bridges seemed uninterested.

The gargoyle was just as ugly as she remembered. Goodman set it down so that it stood facing him, then brought out his wallet. "It looks as though it's the right one, but I must be sure." He took a dark sliver from one of the compartments in his wallet and pressed it against the statue. It was as though it had melted in its hand, merging with the outer shell of the statue without leaving a seam or any other sign that it had once been separate. "It's genuine, Miss Coyne. I can hardly believe it after all this time."

"So where do we go from here? Cut it open?"

Goodman took a deep breath. "Nothing so crude. I have rehearsed this moment so many times that I no longer have to refer to the text. There is an incantation which will cause the statue to reveal its secret."

Goodman's eyes closed and he began muttering almost inaudibly, a repetitious incantation that lasted a full minute before he suddenly stopped. The gargoyle stood where it had been placed, apparently unchanged.

Muscat had been watching intensely, but he suddenly gave a violent shake. "Nothing has happened! You must have gotten the incantation wrong!"

"I made no mistake, you idiot! I know the text better than I know my own name."

"Then the statue is a fake."

Goodman shook his head. "The shaving fit perfectly. It was removed while the gargoyle was in the palace in Malta. Unless the original was stolen and replaced while it was still in the imperial collection."

During the incantation, Wilma had slipped out of the ropes binding her and quietly left the apartment. Only Wanda had noticed until now and she had decided not to intercede. Goodman glanced at the empty chair. "I'm sorry to say that Mr. Muscat and I shall have to leave you in the lurch. You'll have to deal with the suspicions of the local police without a sacrificial lamb." He glanced at Bridges. "Unless you choose to recast the role. I'll trouble you to return the money I gave you last evening."

Wanda crossed her arms and met his eyes. "I provided the goods and earned the money, Mr. Goodman. I see no reason why I should give you a refund."

Goodman's lips thinned. "I paid for the authentic article, not this imitation."

"I'm not sure I recognize the distinction." Wanda reached into her pocket and took out the roll of bills. She counted out half and threw it down onto the table. "But I'm willing to compromise."

Goodman swept up the bills and made them disappear. "Perhaps someday we'll have reason to conduct business again."

"I look forward to it," she lied. Wanda crouched and stared into the gargoyle's ugly face.

And that's when the gargoyle opened its eyes. Wanda met its gaze calmly but Bridges gave a cry of surprise or fright or both and backed away. Goodman and Muscat spun around. "You see!" Goodman's excitement was palpable. "It only took awhile to take effect."

"It's alive!" said Muscat.

"No, not alive. It's just a statue. But it has been animated by the incantation. It will reveal its secret now. It must!"

The gargoyle continued to stare at Wanda as it unfurled two large, batlike wings and stretched its limbs tentatively. Then, before anyone could move, it leaped into the air and began to soar around the room like some oversized, grotesque bat. It made three passes back and forth while the four onlookers ducked away, then headed directly for the nearest window. There was the sound of broken glass and splintering wood and then a cool breeze, but the gargoyle itself was nowhere to be seen.

"I don't understand!" cried Muscat. "Where has it gone?"

Goodman's face cleared. "Of course. How foolish of me. The gargoyle is compelled to reveal the secret to those who wish to see it, but the secret is not here. It must be in Malta."

"Malta!"

"It is undoubtedly on its way to Bocsai's mansion. There it will stand watch until ordered to reveal the secrets of its creator."

"Then we must follow it."

"We will, this very afternoon if we can book passage."

And then they were gone, leaving Wanda alone with her only remaining client.

She ignored Bridges and picked up the phone. Lieutenant Poorhouse was at his desk. "I've got some more info for you." She described Goodman, Muscat, and Wilma Fry and told him where Goodman was staying. "Fry might have split. I took away her gun but she might have another. This one will probably match up with the bullets you dug out of Thursday. Goodman has a daughter but I don't know if she's involved. It was Fry who killed Thursday and the guy in my office, acting on Goodman's orders." She offered a brief outline of the story as far as she knew it, then hung up.

Bridges was staring at her. "They'll implicate us when the police catch them, you know."

"They'll implicate you." Wanda meant it to sound cruel and unfeeling.

"I know I got in over my head, but I also knew Goodman and the others would cut me out of the payoff."

"So explain to me how it all happened. Goodman hired you originally, I gather."

She nodded. "He hired Muscat and I. We hadn't worked together before and I didn't trust him. I was right not to. So I called Thursday and suggested that we play our own hand. If we got the gargoyle first, we could renegotiate terms with Goodman and cut Muscat out completely. Lloyd was good, or lucky, or both. He had some contacts who put us on the right trail and he acquired the statue about a month later."

"He stole it, you mean."

"I'm not sure anyone properly owned it. Joe found it in a mansion in Trieste. No one there had any idea what it actually was." She frowned. "Or what it was supposed to be."

"I don't imagine Muscat was too happy with you."

"He wasn't. He found out what was going on and made threats. Lloyd arranged some difficulties for Joe and he got arrested. But I got nervous. There were rumors that Lloyd had doublecrossed one of his partners a few years back. So I packed up the gargoyle and talked to an old friend about getting it into the States for me."

"That would be Hamut?"

"Yes. I knew about his smuggling business. He breeds salamanders somewhere in Croatia, then sells them all around the world. He promised to deliver my package personally. He was an honorable man in his way. Always insisted upon keeping his word."

"Thursday must have been pissed."

"Only at first. I convinced him that it was a necessary precaution. I was trying to protect myself, not cut him out. We flew back to the States together. All we had to do was wait for *The Dove* to arrive, negotiate a price with Goodman, and complete the deal. But then I found out that Lloyd had talked to Goodman without telling me. I confronted him and he insisted that Goodman had initiated the contact and that he wasn't trying to cut me out. But I wasn't convinced, so I came to you and asked you to follow him. I wanted to know what he was really up to."

"So why did you warn Thursday that he was being followed?"

Bridges recoiled. "I didn't! Why would I do that?"

Wanda sat down in the chair facing Bridges and stared at her. "Matt Bowman was past his prime but he was still a first rate detective. There's no way that Thursday could have spotted him unless he knew what to look for."

"Alright, I wanted to scare him. He'd think twice about a doublecross if there were other eyes watching. But I didn't know that he'd kill your partner. That's the truth."

Wanda nodded. "Thursday didn't kill Matthew."

"But who else could it have been?"

"Matthew would have known that he'd been made. And even if he hadn't, he would never have gone down onto a lonely pier like that. If Thursday had been meeting a boat, there would've been no way for Matthew to follow. If he wasn't, he'd be coming back the same way. You told us Thursday was dangerous but even if you hadn't, there's no way he would have put himself in that kind of danger without a good reason."

"But obviously he did."

Wanda shook her head. "He would have had good reason to think he was safe. No, he wasn't shadowing Lloyd Thursday when he was killed, and he wouldn't have dropped the ball unless our client had called him off. You were our client; you took Matthew out onto that pier and you killed him with a salamander provided by the good services of your friend Hamut."

"You're wrong."

"Save the innocent plea until Poorhouse and his friends get here, which ought to be pretty soon. If we're going to get our story set before they arrive, you'd better start telling me everything right now."

"It's not what you think."

"You don't know what I think, but if you still believe you can get away with lying to me, let's see how well you've done in the past. You moved to the Tiara after someone searched your room at The Golden Dawn, right?"

"Yes, I told you that."

"Then why had you already rented the room at the Tiara three days earlier?"

"I needed some place to go where Lloyd couldn't find me. I was afraid that he'd decide to take all the money for himself."

"The way I see it, you were afraid to go after Thursday yourself. He was wary of you and dangerous. So you decided to provoke something between him and Matthew. If he killed Matthew, you could arrange for the police to get an anonymous tip. On the other hand, if he tried and Matthew killed him instead, you were free to deal with Goodman on your own and pocket the whole reward."

"You don't understand. I was afraid of him. I didn't know what else to do."

"Oh, you found something else. When your first idea didn't pan out, you improvised. You asked Matthew to go out on that pier with you and you killed him. You didn't use a conventional weapon because the cops might have wondered why the bullets didn't come from Thursday's gun. Or maybe you just like burning holes through people's bodies."

"I'm not a monster." Most of the emotion had leeched out of her voice. "I did what I thought I had to do to protect myself."

"I believe you. I really believe that's what you thought."

"Then you'll help me?"

Wanda looked vaguely surprised. "No, of course not. I'm turning you over to the cops. You're lucky; we don't have the death penalty in Massachusetts. If you behave yourself, you might get parole in ten or twenty years."

Bridges stood up and grabbed her bag. "All right, tell them what you want if that's how you feel."

"Where do you think you're going?"

"I have friends here in the city. They'll help me even if you won't."

Wanda stood up slowly. "You're not going anywhere. I'm still potentially on the hook here. If I don't give you up, they still might not be able to pin the job on me, but they'll have my license at least. Sorry, but you're just going to have to face the music."

"You can't stop me from leaving!"

Wanda stepped between Bridges and the door. "Do you want to place a bet on that?"

She didn't.

CHAPTER EIGHTEEN

Poorhouse and Dandy showed up about an hour later. There hadn't been much conversation during the interval. Wanda let them in and turned over Wilma's gun, the firedrake, the shards of the statue that remained, and the charm that had blinded the door guardian. She gave them a quick summation. "I'll come down and do a formal statement later today." Poorhouse had nodded periodically during her recital; Dandy just stood to one side, clearly disappointed that they weren't going to be taking Wanda away in handcuffs.

"You can sweat the parts of the story I don't know from Goodman."

It was Poorhouse's turn to look unhappy. "No, we can't. He was dead when we got there. According to Muscat, the Fry woman was waiting for them. She shot him the minute he walked into the room. She'd already killed the daughter."

"Did you get Wilma at least?"

"She was gone by the time we got there. Muscat was alone with the two bodies, searching the room. He looked genuinely offended when we arrested him. Refuses to say a word, but he'll talk eventually. We'll find the Fry woman sooner or later."

Wanda wasn't so sure, but she let it slide. Instead she told them about Bridges and Matthew Bowman and her connection to Hamut. Poorhouse looked gloomy when he cuffed Bridges but Dandy finally looked cheerier. At least he had arrested someone. Bridges still hadn't said a word when they took her away.

Wanda didn't know how she felt, other than relief that it was all over with. But of course it wasn't. Wilma Fry was still out there somewhere and she seemed the type to hold a grudge. Wanda decided to treat herself to a good steak with some of Goodman's money but she hadn't walked more than a block from her front door when someone tried to kill her.

It was a drive by and not well planned or executed. Wanda never caught even a glimpse of the driver but she recognized the shooter in the split second before she dived dropped behind a parked car, hitting the sidewalk hard enough to leave her breathless. She counted four shots and there was a burning pain in her right hand. At first she thought she'd been hit but it was just fragments of cement kicked up by the closest bullet. The car roared by without stopping, which was a good thing because it was several seconds before the pain subsided enough that she could take out her own weapon. She stayed where she was for another minute, then cautiously stood up. There wasn't much pedestrian traffic and most of it had run off at the first shot. An elderly man called to ask if she was okay and she waved an answer, not trusting her voice just yet.

The shooter had been Wilma Fry. But was she acting on her own – she certainly had good reason for wanting Wanda dead – or had she found a new employer? The last thing Wanda needed now was another distraction. The Willett case was just getting interesting.

Perry had news for her when she finally reached her office. "Guess who I just saw having a friendly lunch together at the Mystical Lounge?"

"An unlikely group, I gather." She sat on the corner of Perry's desk.

"Ezra Willett and Max Taylor. They acted like they were old friends who hadn't seen each other in years."

Wanda pondered that for a moment. "So they've patched up their feud, at least cosmetically. I guess Ezra's filial affection has expired."

"You think Taylor had something to do with his son's death?"

"I don't have an opinion yet, but the old man must have his suspicions. Nathan's secretary is using an assumed name and she's engaged to Myles Lewis, who is the mayor's closest advisor. Taylor and Ezra are involved in most of the shadier business deals in the city. My guess is that Taylor and Diana Marks selected Selma Hairston, now Sharon Llewellyn, to keep an eye on Nathan Willett and that somehow she found herself in position to snag Lewis. Maybe her boss found out something about her and Taylor had him killed. Or maybe she did it herself. I'm pretty sure she tried to kill Diana Marks."

"Why would she do that?"

"If she's going to marry the mayor's assistant, she's going to be in the news. Marks knows about her past. Blackmail would be the next logical step."

"But if she's working for Taylor, why would she be worried about his girlfriend blowing the whistle on her?"

Wanda shrugged. "Maybe she's not as bright as I think she is and she acted on her own. Or maybe Taylor is willing to sacrifice a bishop to gain a rook. He doesn't strike me as the kind who would allow a romance to interfere with business."

"So what would convince Ezra to patch up the old feud just when he had good reason to do the opposite?"

"That is a very good question, to which I have not even a questionable answer. Yet. And we have another problem." She told Perry about the close encounter with Wilma Fry.

He whistled. "There's a woman who holds a grudge."

Wanda stood up. "I have to think a while. Tell the hordes of new clients that show up that I'm gone for the day." And she went into her office and closed the door.

She thought hard all afternoon, barely glancing up when Perry knocked and said he was going home. It was already dark outside. There was the skeleton of a plan in her mind, but only the first steps were clear to her. What happened after that depended upon how the ants reacted when she kicked the anthill. She looked up the number in Perry's rolodex and called Ezra Willett. The secretary did not sound glad to hear from her.

"He's engaged. I can take a message."

"He needs to get disengaged and what I have to tell him is for his ears only." The secretary argued a bit, then finally agreed to find out if Willett was willing to see her. It turned out that he was, though perhaps reluctantly. "Half an hour," Wanda said.

She left through the service entrance, just in case Wilma was lurking out front, and hailed a taxi two blocks away. There was a burly guard on duty at Willett's mansion and he looked at her suspiciously while he called the house, then opened the gate.

Ezra did not look happy when she stepped into his den. He glanced up from some papers he'd been examining and frowned. "I hope you haven't come here to waste my time."

Uninvited as usual, Wanda sat down facing him. "You wanted me to look into your son's death."

"As I recall, you turned me down."

"Maybe I was hasty. And I did say I was going to poke around a bit anyway. I did, and I found out a few things. First of all, your daughter-in-law is Max Taylor's sister."

"I've known that all along. Don't you think that I would have had my son's fiancé's background checked?"

"I assumed you had. I wondered why you hadn't mentioned it when I first came to you."

Willett sighed and leaned back in his chair. "I'm pretty sure I don't like you, Coyne, but I admire your nerve so I'll give you a little history. When Max Taylor came to Boston, I was already well established. If there was a pie, I had a finger in it, whether that pie was legit or not so much. Taylor had similar ambitions and there was a lot of friction. It might have been worse, but he prefers to stay out of the limelight and a full scale war would have brought too much attention. So we had a little get together and we drew some borders and wrote up some rules. My son and his sister met a few times when we all got together and then they started meeting on their own. She wasn't so uptight back then, but she was ambitious and I suspect her brother concocted a little love potion, though I was never able to prove it. I might have looked a little closer, but the marriage had some advantages from my point of view and my son seemed happy – whether it was spontaneous or superimposed – so I played nice."

"You and Taylor became partners?"

He shook his head. "I'm not that nice, or that gullible. But we had a kind of entente. My son, unfortunately, developed some scruples. Must be from his mother's side. He found out something about Taylor, something big, but I don't know what it was. I tried to convince him to forget about it, but he was determined to go public as soon as he had definite proof."

"Did you warn Taylor?"

"Of course not. If Nathan had brought Taylor down, it would have worked to my benefit, and I would not have broken our agreement."

"Which means that Taylor might well have had your son killed."

"Yes, and if you can prove that, I'd be very grateful. Tangibly grateful. But I don't think you can and I'm not entirely certain he was responsible. Nathan had made more than one enemy."

"I understand that you and Taylor have recently had a rapprochement."

The old man moved uncomfortably in his chair. "As I implied, Max has made a convincing argument that he wasn't responsible for Nathan's death."

"Did he suggest an alternative solution?"

"He made a strong case that it was Diana Marks."

Wanda raised an eyebrow. "His girlfriend?"

"Former girlfriend. Max was losing interest and he thinks Marks might have killed Nathan to get back in his good graces. And she's gone into hiding. I checked on her. She is a violent woman and she has almost certainly killed before."

"He might just be casting her as a scapegoat."

"I know that." Willett suddenly looked older, but his voice was firm. "Whether or not his version is the truth, it is to my benefit that I accept it as such."

"Then you don't really want me to look into this any further."

"Oh, but I do. Nathan is gone but I'm still in the game and if you can bring me greater leverage to use against my adversaries, I'd be a fool not to accept it."

Wanda thanked him for his time and left.

She stopped at a bar for a couple of medicinal drinks, then went home. There were two bills in her mailbox; she left them there. When the door imp opened the door for her, a stiff breeze took her by surprise. She had covered over the window where the gargoyle had broken free with a piece of stiff cardboard, but it was hanging by one piece of tape and her apartment was open to the night air. She retrieved the roll of masking tape and climbed up onto a chair, securing it back in place. She would have to get it fixed.

Wanda was about to climb down when she heard something moving in the bedroom. It was just a faint rustle, not particularly furtive, but it definitely didn't belong. Wanda took out her weapon and stepped down cautiously. She doubted Wilma Fry could have gotten past the door imp without damaging it but she could have enlisted the assistance of someone with more formidable skills. The imps were loyal but not particularly bright. Spending their entire lives embedded in a mechanical locking device limited their store of experience.

Wanda found a spot from which she could see the bedroom doorway clearly but where someone coming out would have to waste a second or so looking around to spot her. Then she called out loudly. "I know you're there. Come out slowly and with your hands empty."

There was no response.

Wanda really didn't want to do this right now. She was tired, frustrated, and annoyed that her home had been invaded. It was bad enough that dead men walked into her office and dull witted thugs shot at her from moving cars. Suddenly impatient, she moved quickly across the threshold and called up the lights, arms extended so that her weapon could sweep across the narrow bedroom.

No one was there. She checked the closet and looked under the bed and that was pretty much the only hiding places available. It was only when she started to relax that she noticed that something was on her dresser that didn't belong there. At first it looked like a featureless bronze ball, but then she picked out the details and realized that they were the edges of featherless wings drawn tightly around a small body.

"Well, hello there," she said as she put her weapon away. "What are you doing here?" She crouched down so that her eyes were level with the Maltese gargoyle, which appeared to be curled up and asleep. It didn't react to her voice and after a while she went to bed, deciding to sort things out after a night's sleep.

CHAPTER NINETEEN

The gargoyle was still there when she woke up the following morning, but it had unfurled its wings and shifted position slightly so that it was watching her. She sat up and met its unblinking gaze. She had seen real gargoyles and she knew that her uninvited houseguest was not one of them, not a living thing at all technically. It was essentially a homunculus, though not in human form. It had a purpose and rudimentary instincts, but it was incapable of learning, improvising, or modifying whatever commands had been imposed by its maker.

"Well, little fellow, I hope you had a pleasant night's rest." She got out of bed slowly, not wanting to activate its flight mechanism, but it didn't react at all. "I'm going to have a shower and make some coffee. I don't suppose you drink coffee? No, I didn't think so."

It was still there when she returned from her shower and dressed. It might have been a statue, although she thought its head had turned slightly. She went to the tiny kitchen and brewed coffee and when it was done and she turned around, the gargoyle was on the room divider. "I don't suppose you can tell me what you want." If it could, it chose not to.

Wanda pondered the problem but nothing occurred to her and she had to go to the office. "Well, friend, you're welcome to stay if you want. If not, you already know the way out."

Perry was busy at his desk when she arrived. "We had a visitor last night."

"Oh?" Wanda glanced around but there was no sign of vandalism.

"I found this tucked under the door when I opened up." Perry offered her a small, sealed envelope. There was nothing written on it. "I ran it through the spell senser and it came out green."

Wanda opened it carefully. There was a single, folded piece of white paper inside. "8:00 Tonight. Crowley's Statue. DM" So Diana Marks wanted to meet with her. That was convenient because Wanda wanted to talk to Marks and had no idea where she might be hiding. Apparently she hadn't left Boston. She slipped the note into her pocket. "Anything else brewing?"

"Ava called."

"If she calls back, tell her I died."

"She'd just hire a medium to bug you in the afterlife."

"Probably so. I'm going out for a while."

She had a pretty good idea where she could find the Whisperer. He didn't advertise his involvement with the Grimoire, arguably the most popular night club in Boston, but it wasn't really a secret either. He had an office in the back and he lived in a suite of rooms mounted above the private meeting rooms at the rear. There was no guarantee that he would be there now, of course, but it seemed worth the trip to the north side.

The Grimoire was decorated with arcane symbols but they were decorative rather than functional. The door appeared to be a seven foot tall book with cabalistic calligraphy that did have some functionality – it wouldn't admit minors - and it opened with the sound of rustling pages when anyone entered. The club wasn't open but a youngish man trimming the wolfsbane agreed to see if anyone would speak to her. He returned promptly followed by a neckless goon who told her that Mr. Taylor was not to be disturbed. "He sleeps late."

"I could wait for him to get up. It's important."

"Why would he care?"

"That's for him to decide, don't you think?"

The goon just stared at her and Wanda was about to downgrade her estimate of his intelligence when she realized he was empathically linked to someone inside and was waiting for instructions. "All right. C'mon in."

Half a dozen people were setting tables, mopping floors, or otherwise preparing for the noon opening. The goon led her to a table and told her to stay there and after a few minutes a marginally more polite woman asked if she wanted coffee, which she did. She was working on her second cup when the goon reappeared. "He'll see you now."

Wanda followed him through a brief but bewildering maze of corridors. She should have been able to memorize the route because there were only five turns, but it was all a blur and she realized that a confusion spell concealed the proper route from anyone unauthorized. They came to a door and the goon gestured for her to go inside, but he didn't follow.

The Whisperer was sitting in a lounge chair, dressed in a blue silk robe. He didn't rise but he did invite her to sit in one of the other chairs. She chose a bentwood rocker. "I understand there was some unpleasantness yesterday. I see that you came through it undamaged."

"Now how would you happen to know about that? I didn't notify the police. I don't suppose you were sending me a message?"

"Not I, Miss Coyne. When I send a message, it gets delivered. But in my position, one hears things that might not make it into the public record. Someone doesn't like you."

"A lot of people don't like me. The feeling is mutual."

"Given the low price on the contract, I'm surprised anyone picked it up. You have a somewhat daunting reputation."

Wanda's face was impassive but her mind worked quickly. If someone had advertised for a killer to take her out, then Wilma was probably not just looking to even the score. She would no doubt enjoy her work but money was the motivator. "I didn't come here to talk about my problems. I came to talk about yours."

Taylor looked amused. "I wasn't aware that I had any problems worth talking about. And if I did, why would I discuss them with you?"

"Maybe because I'm the one in the best position to help you." Taylor didn't react, so Wanda pushed on. "Ezra Willett thinks you had his son killed."

"I didn't, and we had a conversation about it. Your information is out of date."

Wanda allowed herself to look amused. "I spoke to him last night and he's not buying the idea that Diana Marks was behind the hit. He hired me to find out the truth."

"And why should I believe you?"

"Because I'm still on the case and there's no one else likely to pay me. Even your sister seems perfectly happy with the outcome."

Taylor suddenly became more alert. "Leave my sister out of this. She's not involved."

"She was married to a man who was about to put a spotlight on her brother's darker side. She had to know at least some of the

details. If she had to choose between her husband and her brother…"
She left the sentence unfinished.

Taylor sat forward suddenly. "Gladys and I used to be close, but we grew apart even before she met Nathan Willett. I doubt that she'd raise a finger to help me." Wanda sensed his uncertainty and decided the seed was firmly planted.

"If I manage to track down Marks, is she going to confirm your story that she acted without your knowledge, had Willett killed just to impress you with her devotion?"

"I can't imagine that she'd admit anything incriminating. That doesn't mean it isn't true."

"What if she agreed to submit to a Truth Search? I know you have influence with the Sorcerers' Council but Baltus the Younger and Lady Bethany would do a fair reading and no one would question what they found. That might be enough that the Council would be forced to compel you to submit to an examination. Particularly if Ezra Willett was pulling a few strings of his own."

Taylor clearly didn't find that idea appealing. "The question is moot unless Marks turns up. By now she could be on the other side of the world."

"It's a small planet."

Taylor swung his feet around and stood up. "I think this conversation is over."

Wanda stood up as well, but she took her time so that he'd know she wasn't intimidated. "Until next time then."

Wanda knew that she would have to move fast if she wanted to widen the gap between Ezra Willett and the Whisperer. Chances were good that they would not confer immediately and discover that she'd been lying to them. Neither man would move until he had time to consider the possible outcomes and initiate measures to contain the problem. Even if they did get together, it was entirely possible that their longstanding rivalry would give legs to their suspicions.

It didn't take very long to find Freddie. Freddie was a rumor processor. He heard so many things and so quickly that there had long been stories that he had a previously unknown magical talent. Wanda didn't believe it. You couldn't necessarily trust what Freddie told you. He had no plausibility filter and would tell you outlandish, even contradictory, bits of gossip during the course of a single conversation. He might be able to tap into the grapevine to a degree impossible for anyone else, but he repeated the true and the false indiscriminately. She had used him before when she wanted something unofficially broadcast citywide but she had never before fed him a deliberate lie.

She found him on the verandah of the Golden Dawn Hotel, sipping his inevitable mint julep and talking to a disreputable looking man with shifty eyes whom Wanda was pretty sure was an undercover cop working in Addictive Spells and Potions. She ordered a glass of tomato juice and drank it until money changed hands and the man left.

"How's business, Freddie?" She took a seat opposite him without being invited. Everyone was welcome at Freddie's table, though some were more welcome than others. Freddie was not a stereotypical snitch. He'd have been good looking if he hadn't accumulated fatty pouches in his cheeks and he wore a tailored suit that probably cost as much as Wanda would make in a good month.

"The information business is always thriving, Coyne. I haven't seen you in a while. On vacation?"

"What's a vacation? I'm looking for someone. Name's Diana Marks. Heard anything lately?" She didn't really expect Freddie to know anything useful. Marks seemed to be acting on her own, and resourcefully. But she needed a good reason to talk to Freddie. He had ethics of a sort and wouldn't pass on the story she wanted spread if he thought she was manipulating him.

"Marks. Girlfriend of the Whisperer." Freddie's eyes lost focus as they usually did when he was perusing his mental files. "Ex-girlfriend, reportedly. Some people think she may have been involved with the hit on Nathan Willett. Interesting past. Worked for Alice Quinn, went off on her own. A couple of people she crossed paths with disappeared suddenly. No one has seen her for a couple of days."

"I already knew all that."

"She might have gone to Nepal, but the evidence is flimsy. She might be dead. I've had two reports that old man Willett had her killed, and another that the Whisperer snuffed her himself so that no one would find out he put her up to it." There was more, some of it wildly improbable, none of the plausible information was new to her.

"How about Wilma Fry?" She might as well find out something useful since she was going to have to pay Freddie anyway.

"Small time thug. Wanted for two counts of murder."

He was going to expand on the crimes but Wanda interrupted. "Anything since she escaped from City Jail?"

"Not much. Did you know there's a price on your head? Fry picked up the contract. Not a very complimentary fee."

"So I've been told. Do you have any idea who placed the order?"

"The name I've heard associated with it is Mason Adams, but he's probably a front."

Wanda frowned. "Never heard of him."

"Another small time thug. Used to work for the Whisperer, but he messed up a lot and was let go."

"Why would he have it in for me?"

Freddie shrugged. "Haven't heard a thing. He's a loner. Doesn't talk much."

"Any idea who' s behind him?"

"Not a glimmer."

Once she was convinced that Freddie had nothing more to give her, Wanda put some money on the table but made no move to leave. "I imagine you've heard about the feud between old man Willett and the Whisperer."

"The word is they kissed and made up."

"I understand that was all for show. Willett doesn't believe the story that Marks killed his son without Taylor knowing about it, and the two of them are still tussling over control of the waterfront."

Freddie leaned forward like an addict waiting for his next fix. "The word on the street is that they reached an amicable understanding."

"They're just posing to put each other off balance. If that was the case, why would Willett be paying me to find out who killed his son and steering me toward Taylor? If he believed it was Marks, he'd be a lot more interested in finding her."

Freddie mulled that one over.

"And I also heard that Taylor has visitors from New Orleans."

Freddie blinked rapidly. "The Whisperer has never used voodoo before. It's not his style."

"Which would make him look less suspicious if zombie goons knocked off Willett or some of his key people."

"Something like that might even make the Council sit up and take notice. Voodoo is banned within metropolitan limits except by special license."

"The Whisperer sits on the Council, remember? And he has a lot of influence. If he wants something squashed or just misdirected, he's in a perfect position to do so." That was enough. Anything further and Freddie might get suspicious. She pushed back her chair and sat up. "You didn't hear any of that from me."

"Of course not. I never divulge my sources. You know that."

She did. In fact, she was counting on it.

By late afternoon she'd talked to two more snitches, neither as reliable as Freddie. She added slight variations to the story, and when Freddie got wind of them he'd add them to his inventory. It wouldn't be long before things started to percolate.

She went back to the office and found Poorhouse talking to Perry.

"I thought you might want to know that Fry is still in the city. She was spotted by one of our undercover people. He called it in but he couldn't do it right away and she was gone before we arrived."

"I'm disappointed in you, Poorhouse. She's hardly the master criminal type and she's a stranger in town."

"Well, she's made at least one friend. She was with another hood when she was spotted."

"Anyone I know?"

"Possibly, but he's a bottom feeder. Guy by the name of Mason Adams."

Wanda nodded. "Used to work for Max Taylor."

"An old friend?"

"No, a new enemy. I think I had a recent close encounter with the two of them." She described the shooting incident.

"You know you're really supposed to report something like that to the police." Poorhouse played it mock stern.

"I was going to but something came up and it happens so often that I didn't think it was particularly important."

Poorhouse told her to watch her back and went away. Perry waited until he was gone. "Do you have a plan yet?"

"Yes."

"Is it a good one?"

"All my plans are good ones. It's not my fault when people don't act the way I expected them to." She looked around at the dingy office, which seemed unusually repellent. "Let's call it a day."

Wanda went home to eat. As soon as she was inside her door she glanced up at the patched window. The cardboard was still in place so her visitor was still around. It took a minute to find the gargoyle, which was now perched on an end table. Its wings were furled but its eyes were wide open and staring roughly in her direction. She waved to it and went to the kitchen, making herself a tuna fish sandwich even though the bread was slightly stale. The preservation spell on the breadbox had expired a month earlier.

She had eaten half of it when she noticed that the gargoyle had moved. It was now sitting on the couch beside her. Its wings were swept back down and the head was upturned so that it stared at her face. "So what can I do for you, little fellow?" Wanda didn't expect an answer so when she got one, sort of, she almost choked on a mouthful of tuna.

The gargoyle raised its wings above its head and thrust its chest forward. As it did so, the toro opened vertically along some invisible seam to reveal a hollow interior. There was just enough light that she could see a very small scroll tucked diagonally into the space. She reached for it tentatively, half expecting to be resisted, but the gargoyle remained motionless until she plucked it out. Then the compartment closed, the wings curled up around the body, and the eyes closed. It looked like any other inanimate statue.

The scroll was made entirely from gold, pressed thin enough that it could be rolled up like a piece of parchment. It bore several dozen lines of text, all inscribed by hand. They were in Latin, which she couldn't read. Wanda rolled it up carefully and carried it out to the kitchen. The wine rack, which had been empty for a long time, had a false bottom and she placed the scroll inside. Then she finished her sandwich and started out to meet Diana Marks.

CHAPTER TWENTY

The statue of Aleister Crowley stood in a small graveyard in a part of Boston that had once been genteel but was now hovering on the brink of slumdom. Wanda arrived forty-five minutes early because she wanted to scout the area beforehand. She had no way of knowing for certain that Diana Marks had actually sent the message, and even if she had, it would be to the advantage of some people if the two of them never left the graveyard alive, if at all.

She walked through the adjacent blocks and saw only a handful of people. Two giggling teenagers walked briskly past her and one made a muffled comment that was almost certainly about her, but she ignored it. There was a homeless man sleeping in a doorway. He looked authentic, but masking spells were very hard to penetrate with the unaided senses. She wouldn't forget about him. A bus drove past but didn't stop. There was a bar open facing away from the cemetery and she went inside and had a glass of wine. She was the only customer and the bartender, a young man with unruly hair and a bad complexion, was clearly more interested in a mechanical game of fairy chess than in his job.

No one entered or departed from the cemetery. Wanda made a quick pass through, then found herself a shadowy place to wait near the periphery. Just before eight, someone appeared at the gate at the far end, hesitated for a long time, then slipped inside. It appeared to be a man with a slouch hat, carrying a shovel, and Wanda would have thought him to be a caretaker, except that caretakers didn't work in the evening.

She stayed where she was until the figure approached the state of Crowley and stopped there, looking around. Wanda put a hand into her pocket, found her weapon, and held it out of sight when she stepped forward. "Hello, there! Looking for me?"

The figure straightened and turned toward Wanda, staring as she came closer. She was almost within arm's reach when it abruptly collapsed into dust with the faintest whisper of sound. Wanda stopped where she was, blinking, and her weapon came out of her pocket, but then a familiar voice spoke out of the darkness.

"You won't need that. It was just a dust wraith. I wasn't going to manifest myself until I knew there wasn't a sensitive waiting to track my aura. "The statue of Crowley stirred and turned to face her. "You didn't really expect me to show up physically, did you?"

Crowley was a stern faced, older male and the feminine voice was anachronistic. Wanda hadn't tagged Marks as capable of something like that, but she had been dating an accomplished sorcerer for a while and must have picked up some trick. "Remote projection. I'm impressed. I didn't know you had magical talents."

"They're marginal but I always keep a couple of augmentation spells around. They come in handy for occasions like this."

"So why not just manifest yourself in my office?"

"Your building is warded. I could get past the barrier but it would take some effort and this place appealed to my sense of the theatrical."

"So why am I here?"

"I understand I'm supposed to have hired someone to kill Nathan Willett."

"I've heard rumors to that effect."

"You know where the rumors originated, don't you?"

Wanda could think of no good reason to conceal what must be common knowledge. "The Whisperer. A lovers' quarrel?"

"We were intimate but there was no love involved. Do you think Max had him killed?"

Wanda shrugged. The statue was more than life sized and she had retreated a few steps instinctively. "I haven't developed an opinion yet. What's your theory?"

"It wouldn't surprise me. I'm pretty sure that Willett, the younger one, had evidence linking him to Ryan Newland."

Newland had been Ezra Willett's major competitor until his unsolved murder several years earlier, just about the time Max Taylor moved to Boston and before he had been appointed to the Council. Newland's penthouse had ceased to exist late one night while Newland was conducting a meeting with several of his lieutenants. None of them had ever been seen again.

"Newland was a very influential man. He had links to a lot of people."

"Not very many of them could carry off a compression spell."

Wanda nodded to herself. There were several plausible theories about what had happened to the one time crime boss, but her favorite was that the entire penthouse, and its contents, had been magically squeezed down to the size of a dust mote, which would have been blown away by the evening breeze.

"That would be hard to prove. No physical evidence."

"There might be. What would you say if I told you that Max had an amulet that was magically bound shut, and that he opened it once to show me what was inside? A tiny fleck of dust."

"I'd say he was taking a terrible risk."

"I'm not a sensitive, Coyne, but I'm a very perceptive woman. I had a feeling that Max was going to dispense with me, probably before he realized it himself. It can be very dangerous to be one of his former friends, so I picked up some insurance the last time I was at his place. And I left a pretty close duplicate so chances are that he doesn't even know it's gone."

"Sounds like a valuable bargaining chip."

The statue shook its head. "Max might negotiate at gunpoint but he'd never rest easy until he'd gotten back at me. I need to have him brought down."

"So why not turn the evidence over to the police, or the Council? If it is what you say it is, another sorcerer could open it and they could scry out the person responsible. He might survive a trial by the civil authorities but the Council would insist upon life imprisonment in Alcatraz." No magic of any kind would work on the prison island.

"Max has allies on the Council and employees in the police. I can't take the risk. I was kind of hoping you would act as my agent."

"What's in it for me?"

"My heartfelt gratitude is probably not enough, but there is still a substantial reward for anyone who brings Newland's killer to justice. It's all yours if you do me this favor."

"All right, but there's a condition."

Aleister Crowley's perpetual frown deepened. "What kind of condition?"

"You give me the amulet, but I decide just when to bring him down. I have another iron in the fire just now."

"You want Willett's killer. It was probably Max."

"Probably, but not definitely. I need time to find out the truth."

"I can't wait too long. I have strong protection here, but Max is patient and thorough and very talented. Sooner or later, he'll find me."

"Can you hold out for another week?"

The statue was silent for several seconds. "I think so. But that's as long as I'm willing to wait. After that, I'll have to make other arrangements."

"So when do I get the amulet?"

"Tomorrow. I'll have it delivered to your office. Watch for the florist."

Wanda was about to ask another question, but the statue had returned to its original position and instantly became solid and inanimate.

So she went home instead.

It was Friday morning. Wanda reached the office before Perry for a change and was waiting when he came in. "That's for you." She pointed to a pile of bills on his desk. "I think that covers what I owe you."

Perry put the money in his pocket without counting it. "I'm sure it is."

"How much does a translation spell go for nowadays?"

Perry thought about it. "Depends. A general one covering standard languages can go for several hundred."

"I know the language I want translated. Latin."

"They're not much. Maybe ten bucks."

Wanda counted her remaining cash out and pulled out a ten. There wasn't much left, but it would last for a week or two if she was careful. "Here. Pick one up for me when you're not overwhelmed by new clients."

"How'd it go last night?"

"Interesting."

"That could be good, or it could be bad."

"Exactly what I was thinking."

Wanda picked up the morning's *Boston Sphere* from Perry's desk and took it into her office to read. She had heard about the shooting on the waterfront on her radio already and she read the story with considerable interest. Something had sparked an altercation between some of Willett's heavies and the employees of a fish market owned by one of the Whisperer's proxies. Willett controlled the longshoremen and the big distributors, but Taylor's organization had gobbled up the smaller fry. This was the main area of tension between the two empires. Taylor was more interested in magical addictives, pornographic illusion parlors, compulsive love potions, and things of that nature. He controlled, directly or indirectly, a dozen or more restaurants and nightclubs, all of which served as distribution centers. Willett was more mundane and traditional. He pretty much controlled drugs and prostitution citywide, as well as a somewhat gentrified protection racket.

The story in the paper made it sound spontaneous, and maybe it was, but she had planted the rumor two days ago and Wanda rather hoped that Willett had heard the voodoo rumors and was firing a warning shot that he wasn't about to be pushed around.

She leafed through the rest of the paper and saw that Myles Lewis and Sharon Llewellyn had finally tied the knot.

Wanda fiddled with one of the knobs on one leg of her battered desk. There was a click and a piece of the carving swung to one side revealing a hollow space. She took out the amulet that had been delivered in a bouquet of lilies the day after her meeting with Marks, stared at it for a moment, then returned it and closed the compartment. The cache was purely mechanical. Magic concealment could be detected by Finders so she never trusted them. She had four days left in which to use the amulet, but she didn't want to remove Taylor from the game and leave Ezra Willet to sweep the board. The pot was beginning to bubble but it showed no sign of coming to an active boil. And she still didn't know who had murdered Nathan Willett.

On the plus side, no one had tried to kill her recently. Poorhouse had called to say that they were pretty sure Wilma Fry had left Boston, but even if that were true, there was nothing preventing her from coming back. Mason Adams was also among the missing. But the contract was presumably still out there.

She had picked up a new client the day before. It was a routine skip trace and Wanda already had a pretty good idea where her quarry was. It wouldn't do to turn him up too quickly though. She wanted at least a couple of days' worth of fees and expenses.

She had planned to wait one more day but the office was empty and she was restless.

"I'm going out to find Mr. Costello," she told Perry.

Tony Costello had talked a small bank into giving him a business loan and had set up a pizza joint a few too many blocks from the Common to command much of a clientele. A month earlier, the storefront windows had been covered over with butcher's paper and a hand scrawled note indicating that they were redecorating and would reopen in two weeks. Four weeks had passed with no signs of life and the bank contacted the owner of the building who had let them inspect the property.

Needless to say, everything had been taken away – ovens, racks, cash register, tables, chairs, even the menus.

Wanda had found out where the equipment had gone less than an hour after accepting the job. Terry Wainwright was one of Ezra Willett's people. He was ostensibly a scrap dealer but in fact he made a good living redistributing unlikely stolen goods that ordinary fences would laugh off. Restaurant equipment, machine tools, and construction equipment were his bread and butter.

There were two pizza ovens sitting in his warehouse. Since Wanda hadn't been hired to find the equipment, just the delinquent entrepreneur, she had negotiated with Wainwright. She wouldn't say anything to the bank about his latest acquisition if he told her the circumstances under which it had come into his possession.

He had paid cash, of course, which was untraceable. But he hadn't been able to come up with the total for Costello immediately and had instead sent him a bundle of bills the following day. Wainwright gave Wanda the address.

"But I don't know if he's still there."

He was.

Costello hadn't used his own name but he was the only single male recently registered at the badly misnamed Lucky Charms, a deteriorating flophouse on the south side. Wanda would confirm his identity today, take a couple of pictures if possible, and then inform her client.

But she had an errand to run first.

It took a while to find chicken feet at Faneuil Hall Market but a Vietnamese butcher sold her a small package. Wanda tied them together with some twine, added some colorful feathers, a wooden carving of a homunculus designed to go on a keychain, and a couple of dried peppers. She didn't know the first thing about voodoo but she figured Ezra Willlett wouldn't know much more. She wrapped her creation in tissue paper, placed it inside a gift box, then a remailer, and dropped it off at the post office.

Then she went to the Lucky Charms.

She never did figure out whether they had followed her there or somehow anticipated where she was going, but the ambush was sprung as she was easing herself down behind some scruffy bushes growing on an abandoned lot diagonally across from the flophouse, camera at the ready. They came at her from two directions.

She didn't recognize the man on her right, but the firedrake in his hand was all she needed to know. Wanda threw herself to the ground while wrestling out her own weapon just as Wilma Fry stepped out of a doorway to her left. The building itself was a derelict so she must have forced the door because there had been no one standing there when Wanda had passed by a minute or two earlier.

The bushes were dry and they burst into flame when the firedrake discharged. Wanda ignored the flash of heat and fired three shots blindly, her eyes dazzled by the discharge. She had no time to determine whether or not she'd hit her target or at least driven him to cove because she was rolling to one side and turning toward Fry. There was a loud bang and dirt spattered only inches from her face.

She fired one shot in response but knew it was well off target even as she pulled the trigger. It might at least cause Fry to hesitate. There was no cover within reach except the skeleton of a long abandoned Merlin sedan so she gathered her legs under her and sprinted toward it. Another shot rang out and she braced herself but Wilma was apparently not the best shooter in the world because it was another miss.

Sheltered behind the wreck, Wanda glanced back to the right but there was no sign of her other assailant. That might be good news or not. Fry had backed off around the corner of the building but Wanda could see her shadow stretched across the broken sidewalk. She fired one round that ricocheted off the wall less than a foot from where Fry's head presumably was, then reloaded.

It was a standoff. There was insufficient cover for Fry to approach from any other direction, and Wanda had no place to go but could stay right where she was in relative safety. She was less worried about the firedrake, which would need an hour to recharge, but its bearer might be otherwise armed as well. Unless it was something considerable more formidable, he was similarly stymied.

"I thought we were friends, Wilma," she called out.

There was no answer but the shadow moved slightly. Time was on Wanda's side. Sooner or later someone would call the police. This would occur to Fry before long if it hadn't already. Wanda cautiously moved along the side of the sedan so that she could look for Fry's partner. She spotted him. He was lying prone and he wasn't moving, so at least one of her wild shots had struck home.

"Your buddy there doesn't look too well," she called out. "Maybe you should call him a doctor."

Fry shouted an obscenity and suddenly the shadow was gone. Wanda edged back the way she had come, briefly showed her head. No one took a shot at it. She waited a while longer, then bolted toward the remains of the bush where she'd first planned to hide herself. There was no response, but she heard a motor start somewhere in the distance and move off. It seemed a safe bet that Wilma Fry was gone again.

She retrieved her camera from where it had fallen and walked cautiously over to the fallen man. There was a dark hole in his temple and she congratulated herself even though it had been blind luck. Then she checked for a wallet, found one, and read the identification. Mason Daniel Adams, the man who had taken out a contract on her life, was no longer a factor.

At that very moment, a cab drove up to the Lucky Charms and Tony Costello came out of his room and walked over to it. Wanda raised the camera to snap a picture of him just before he got into the cab, but she'd broken the lens when she dropped it. Good luck rarely came unmixed with the bad.

On the way back to her office, she heard on the radio that the mayor had had a fatal accident in his swimming pool. Myles Lewis was now acting mayor.

Wanda was home alone two nights later when the news she'd been waiting for broke on the radio. She had borrowed a camera from Perry earlier that day and – after three boring hours crouched in the bushes – she had a picture of Tony Costello standing under the neon sign for Lucky Charms. The bank was happy – or at least satisfied – and she had cashed their check already.

Captain Dandy had been brusque but only mildly offensive when he'd questioned her about the shooting at the Lucky Charms. The death of Mason Adams had closed one of his open cases for him. "Too bad you didn't get them both."

Perry had picked up the Latin translation spell – actually a pair of charmed reading glasses that would allow her to see the printed text in English – but she had been strangely reluctant to use it. If the scroll held the secret of transmutation, she had the key to riches in her grasp. Although she had no magical talent herself, she could undoubtedly sell or license the secret to someone who could make it work and they would both be very rich very quickly. It was tempting, but Wanda realized that she rather liked her life the way it was. Sure, it would be nice not to be in debt all of the time, but wealth in large quantities changed things dramatically

So she put the glasses in a drawer and told the gargoyle to stick around. It seemed perfectly content to do so, although it moved around the apartment almost every day while she was gone.

She'd gotten into the habit of listening to the radio in the evenings ever since her television had stopped working. There was an all-news station whose repetitive drone she found almost soothing. The information in their stories generally entered her mind through osmosis rather than attentiveness but she stopped what she was doing immediately when the announcer began talking about the fire.

It was the Grimoire, the nightclub where she'd met with Max Taylor, the place where he lived, and the police were already saying that the circumstances were suspicious. There was no report of fatalities, at least not yet. Taylor had not been present at the time of the fire.

Taylor didn't take long to strike back, although it was not clear if Ezra Willett's death was a direct or indirect result of the counterattack. Just before dawn the following morning, there was an armed assault on Willett's mansion. Although he had beefed up his security dramatically, the perimeter was breached in multiple places. The attackers used confusion spells to disorganize the defenders, conventional explosives to open gaps in the walls, and a mix of magical and mundane weapons to slaughter the second line of defenders.

Willett, of course, was hustled into a concealed escape tunnel but he was unconscious and unresponsive by the time his party reached the underground safe room and he died before the siege was lifted. An autopsy was pending but it appeared to have been heart failure. Among the dignitaries interviewed by the media was Max Taylor, who eloquently praised his "old friend" and denied vehemently that he had any knowledge of who might be responsible for the attack.

The following morning, Wanda made an appointment to see Lady Bethany of the Sorcerers' Council and removed the amulet from its hiding place. Lady Bethany had been the only person to vote against Max Taylor's elevation to the Council and she listened with barely concealed delight to Wanda's story.

"I will need to subject this to some tests before I can act on your information," she said quietly, but without concealing her satisfaction. "I hope that your source is trustworthy."

"So do I," admitted Wanda.

But late the following day, word spread through the grapevine that the Whisperer had been taken into joint custody by the Council and the metropolitan police. Diana Marks would still need to watch her step for a while, but it seemed likely she could come out of hiding.

Acting Mayor Lewis had ordered that a task force look into the influence of organized crime in the city. He denied reports that his wife had left him, but Wanda figured that Sharon/Selma had realized that without Max to protect her, she had no way to prevent Diana Marks from telling what she knew.

CHAPTER TWENTY ONE

Wanda still didn't know who had killed Nathan Willett, but she was starting not to care. Her other worry had taken care of itself. Wilma Fry had been arrested when she tried to hold up the wrong convenience store. The clerk had triggered a frosting spell and he, two customers, and Wilma had been frozen solid until it had expired, by which time the police were waiting to arrest Fry. It was unlikely she would be allowed to escape a second time.

Which left Wanda with one problem remaining to be resolved – the scroll she'd removed from the gargoyle. It was sitting on her kitchen table, between the charmed spectacles and the immobile gargoyle. Come what may, Wanda was determined to face up to the issue. She had, in fact, picked up the spectacles and was preparing to put them on when the door imp announced that she had a visitor.

"A woman is approaching your door."

"Has she been here before?"

"No." Wanda breathed easier. At least it wasn't Wilma Fry on the loose again. And it couldn't be Ava because the imp would have recognized her. Diana Marks seemed the most likely candidate.

But it wasn't Diana Marks who had come to call. It was Gladys Willett.

"May I come in? I need to talk to you."

She refused the offer of coffee and didn't spare the gargoyle or the scroll a second look when they sat down at the table.

Wanda felt ill at ease. "I haven't had much luck solving your husband's murder, I'm afraid. But I promise you I haven't forgotten about it. I suspect the triggerman was named Adams, but he's dead now and isn't going to be telling anyone the truth."

"I'm sure you did everything you could."

"I heard about your brother's difficulties." Wanda couldn't bring herself to express any sorrow.

"Maxwell was always brilliant, even as a child, and very talented. Sometimes he acted as though no one could ever touch him and I guess it was inevitable that he'd make a mistake that he couldn't cover up."

"Everyone makes mistakes sooner or later."

"I suppose they do." Gladys seemed more composed than the first time they'd met. Wanda wondered if it was some kind of numbing shock or if she had found some inner strength with which to deal with her problems. "Actually, Max made two of them. The first was to trust that whore, Diana Marks."

Wanda felt a twinge of uneasiness. "Sometimes men prefer to think with something other than their brains."

"I told him that he was making a mistake. But he never listens to me."

Wanda made a sympathetic noise and wondered where this was going. "Was there a reason you came to see me?"

But Gladys ignored her. "His second mistake was even bigger. I told him to do something about that one as well, but he thought I was exaggerating the danger. I didn't need magic to tell me that he should have had you killed right at the start." And Gladys took out a dragon's tooth and let Wanda see it.

"That's a very dangerous thing you have there," said Wanda slowly and as calmly as she could manage.

"She came to see me this morning. The whore, I mean. She wanted to gloat, I guess. I told her to stay away from my brother when they first started seeing each other but she wouldn't listen. She laughed at me. She's not laughing now." Gladys raised her hand. "And she won't ever be laughing again, at me or anyone else."

"What do you want from me, Gladys? It's not my fault that your husband is dead and your brother is going to be locked away for the rest of his life." Well, not entirely.

"Nathan? He was just like you, sticking his nose where it didn't belong. He knew that Maxwell was my brother but that didn't stop him from poking and prying until he found something that would bring down a better man than he ever was. It was inevitable, I suppose. He and the old man might not have been the best of friends but blood is thicker than water. If he'd been the honest crusader that he claimed to be, he could have ruined his father a lot more easily than Maxwell. He knew lots of things that he wouldn't talk about, even to me."

"So your brother was just defending himself, is that it?"

"Maxwell didn't have Nathan killed. Oh, he might have under ordinary circumstances, but he has a strong sense of family – we both do - and Nathan was my husband. He asked me to intercede for him and I tried, but Nathan just got up on his high horse and insisted that he had an obligation to print the truth and he wouldn't suppress it even for my sake. So I looked up an old friend who used to work for Maxwell back before I was even married. He'd always had a crush on me and he was happy to help. Nathan had some money stashed away for emergencies. He didn't think I knew about it, but I did. It's funny in a way. He paid for his own murder. Mason found it quite amusing."

"You paid Mason Adams to kill your own husband?"

"Of course. I didn't have any choice. You're a smart woman. Surely you can see that."

"Yes, I guess I do." Wanda was unarmed, her handgun sitting on the dresser in her bedroom. She had to keep the woman talking and hope that some opportunity offered itself. "You know Adams is dead?"

"I know that you killed him. Don't worry. I wasn't fond of him and this way he won't be telling any tales out of school. You did me a favor there."

"I'd be happy to call us even."

"Oh, we will be before I leave, I promise you. This will also save me some money."

Wanda frowned, but then realized what Gladys meant. "It was you who took out a contract on me."

"Of course, although Mason fronted for me. I thought you'd drop your investigation into Nathan's murder when no one was willing to pay you, but you didn't so I had to do something. I could hardly hire you to not investigate, now could I? I disliked you the moment we met, you know. You're a woman but you try to do a man's job. That's just not right. And then when the whore told me how you'd helped her ruin Maxwell, I just had no other choice. I had to take matters into my own hands."

The dragon tooth came up and Wanda realized there was nothing she could do to stop it. And then something dark crossed her line of vision just as the tooth began to flash and there was an almost silent explosion of light. A pressure wave knocked her off the chair and the back of her head struck the room divider hard enough to stun her for a few seconds.

Desperation gave her the strength to move and she staggered to her feet, prepared to fight or run for the bedroom, whichever seemed the best bet. But she had no need to do either.

Gladys Willett was sprawled backward in her chair. Her eyes were open but they were empty. The gargoyle claws were deeply embedded in her throat and the only reason that her blood wasn't spraying out was that the wound had been cauterized by the backlash from the dragon tooth. The discharge had hit the homunculus squarely in its midsection and whatever magic lent it life was not strong enough to protect it from so powerful a destructive force. A gaping hole had been burnt almost all the way through its body. One wing was gone and the other truncated. The lower part of the head had melted.

It had given its life – or what passed for life – to save her and Wanda had no idea why.

She told the police pretty much the truth. Dandy threatened to have her license for possession and use of unauthorized dangerous magical artifacts, but he seemed to be going through the motions. He would have gloated more if he had thought the charges would stick.

Wanda cleaned up the kitchen after they'd removed the body. They had also taken what remained of the gargoyle and she realized she was going to miss it. She'd gotten used to having it around.

With a fresh cup of coffee, she sat down and once again regarded the scroll and the translation glasses. "What the hell," she said out loud and put them on. Then she began to read.

"To whoever first meets the gaze of Skaith, here is revealed the legacy of George Bocskai, the Alchemist."

The next dozen lines were autobiographical and matched what Wanda had been told about the presumed creator of the gargoyle, identified as Skaith. Bocskai apparently created Skaith to be his bodyguard and to protect his household from thieves.

"Know then that the secret of transmutation has been revealed to me, a secret which has enabled me to live a life of seclusion and study. Wisdom suggests that the possessor of great wealth or of the secret to obtaining it would do well to conceal his good fortune lest it attract the undesired attention of the envious. As I near the end of my life, I find that my early resolve to let this knowledge die with me has withered and I wish now that it survive in some fashion as a hidden but enduring testament to my accomplishments."

There was a list of other magical achievements, most of which were now – if not commonplace – at least far more familiar than they would have been during Bocskai's lifetime. That was followed by cautions about the use of the secret of transmutation. If word of its discovery spread, the value of gold would fall, so the reader was cautioned to create only as much as was needed to support a comfortable lifestyle. Wanda was getting toward the end of the scroll and began to wonder if Bocskai had ever gotten around to actually including the secret. But there it was at last.

"The spell of transmutation has been embodied in Skaith. He will only perform this service for the one whose visage he first sees when he is awakened. Simply place the object to be transformed into the cavity in Skaith's chest. It will remain closed for a day and a night and when it reopens, behold, it will contain the selfsame object, but now composed of solid gold. This is the final gift of the greatest of all thaumaturgs, Bocskai the Immortal."

That was it. No incantation. No occult formula. Nothing at all. Bocskai had embedded his knowledge within the physical form of a gargoyle, and Skaith had been destroyed protecting Wanda, whom it accepted as its new owner.

Wanda leaned back and thought about it. And then she laughed, quite a long time in fact. It looked like she'd have to go on working for a living after all.

She felt quite relieved.